WORDS THAT HURT YOU

MISSION 14

BLACK OCEAN: PASSAGE OF TIME

J.S. MORIN

Magical Scrivener Press
www.magicalscrivener.com

Publisher's Note: This is a work of fiction. Names, characters, places, and incidents are a product of the author's imagination. Locales and public names are sometimes used for atmospheric purposes. Any resemblance to actual people, living or dead, or to businesses, companies, events, institutions, or locales is completely coincidental.

Ordering Information: Special discounts are available on quantity purchases by corporations, associations, and others. For details, contact the publisher at the address above.

J.S. Morin — First Edition

WORDS THAT HURT YOU
MISSION 14

THE HALLWAYS STRETCHED off in two directions, much like time, now that Eric thought about it. Jessie's door, at his back, was a side trip, nothing more. So much more time lay ahead than behind, but all the *stuff* took place in the past. Future history hadn't been written yet...

But at least two days' worth was available in an early draft form.

Eric had seen it.

Eric had lived it.

Could Eric change it?

He verged on answering one of chronomancy's fundamental questions: can you alter the past?

Well, it didn't honestly seem like Eric was *in* the past. The future had just decided to try again.

This was a second chance. Not a second chance like getting picked for kickball after clearly costing his team a win the previous day, or even a second chance to declare his opinion on Charlotte's weird new hairdo. An actual, wipe-the-slate-clean do-over of two whole days.

In theory.

Eric would be operating on a *lot* of theory going forward.

The first thing he needed to check was just how much free will he had. Interrupting Jessie in her quarters hadn't happened last time, but it also was unlikely to have played a significant role in the outcome of Dad's dea—Dad's little incident of not living anymore.

No. This wasn't going to work if Eric couldn't admit what hasn't've will happened.

Dad willn't have died.

There. He'd thought it out loud.

Or, given the state of things, had Dad going to will have died?

Dad wasn't going to die.

Not this time. Not on Eric's watch. He just needed to find out where things went wrong before and fix them.

Easy.

⸻

Wizard Sparta Dahl had spent the last hour or so—though she hadn't set an hourglass—frolicking in bed with her lover, the mighty Hadrian The Brown. In her present exertions, she leaned both hands on his shoulders for support and leverage. There was little fat or flab, though she'd never have considered him muscular, merely "firm" and pleasant and reassuring. Though he'd have resisted any such suggestion of pointless athletic showboating, she imagined he could have run marathons if he put in a modicum of effort.

He certainly seemed to have the endurance for it.

She'd prolonged this encounter, as she had so many others, by engaging his mind in mundanities. Not that he was ever quick, but she could get so much more out of him if they weren't dragging one another toward their inevitable conclusions with every little twitch and gasp. Today's topic had been a delightful back-and-forth on the benefits of tesud cuisine...

Hadrian could be a formidable debater when he chose, but this wasn't his arena for conflict. "Fair enough. Just... let's see... about how often we eat salad."

"I could definitely—" Sparta's whole body stiffened, and her mind clung to the insides of her skull as a torrent of visions washed past her.

"If you need me to move my fingers, I can certainly—"

"Shush," she scolded. So long as he kept some kind of grip on her—any kind at all—she felt moored to reality. "Don't move." She waited for the flurry to pass, then slumped in relief. "That was just the most intense feeling of déjà vu."

"Didn't think I was being that repetitive."

Sparta shook her head, raining a few droplets of sweat. She took a heaving breath. "No. It's not your fault. I don't know what it was other than distracting."

"Can you describe it?"

She considered. Analogies were *his* specialty, and she'd been trying to match him in vividness. "If normal déjà vu is someone shouting your name, this is receiving an ovation for a nightclub act."

Hadrian grunted in amusement. "Didn't hear a lot of those, traveling with Carl's band."

"Well, I need a very specific form of distraction, if you don't mind. Hadrian, could you be a darling and squelch my magic?"

"I thought you hated that."

"Granted. But what I've discovered I hate even more is feeling an oncoming climax and having it slapped aside by my premonitions. Make a game of it. Get on top of me, smother my magic, pin me with your own if you like, and do whatever you like with me."

Sparta was a coiled and wound spring, compressed and jammed inside a gizmo, unable to pop free. She needed help, and this was all she could think to ask.

Hadrian smirked. "Letting you have your way *is* what I like. Call it the privilege of power."

Afterimages swam behind her eyes. Hadrian was out of phase, a drunk-vision blur unable to resolve itself into a single lover.

She laid a finger on his lips to beg for a moment's silence. "Hadrian. This is a favor. I'm not often overwhelmed by my foresight. I just need you to shut the lights off and lead me out of it by the hand. So stop being a studly gentleman and become a rakish cad. Don't answer. If you consent, just throw me down and take me. Magically. Physically. Everything. Just..."

Hadrian widened his eyes. A question? A confirmation?

Sparta nodded. "Do it."

Gravity itself unraveled. Downward became arbitrary. A smothering will overpowered her. If her visions had been a tide, she'd never have imagined sand enough to sop up the very sea itself. But this was Hadrian The Brown, and he was mightier than titans; surely Poseidon could pose no challenge.

He was everything Sparta needed.

A new tide, this one of ecstasy, washed her away.

⸻

Eric strolled the *Arete*, trying to recall all he'd done in the two days leading up to Dad's near-time-travel experience.

For starters, if he was going to get back into the ruts of his wagon ride, he'd eaten that plate of pancakes. Circling back, he discovered that Uom'pe had left his place setting and replaced the fork.

"Thanks for not clearing the dishes," he called out as he took his seat.

"You do. This. More often. Than you. May realize," Uom'pe replied from the kitchen.

Eric lifted the edge of his plate and slipped out the warming disk underneath. The fact that he knew to check there lent credence to Uom'pe's theory. The coffee cup was empty, but a heated carafe beside it offered a self-service option that Eric employed in lieu of bothering the cook, who'd been so kind already.

Cream.

Sugar.

More sugar.

Eric dug in. The pancakes were worse for the wait but still good enough to enjoy. Without a whole lot of decision-making involved in the eating process, he plotted his next move.

His first thought was an obvious one.

This whole business needed to get off the ship faster. Zippity-zip. Move-move-move. And a whole bunch of Mom's other motivational speeches.

Jessie had always been the problem. Once someone told Eric where he needed to be, that was fine. Ozzy, well, most of Eric's childhood, Ozzy had been an even smaller child; half the time, picking him up and carrying him was Mom's solution. But Jessie had her own way of doing things for as long as Eric could remember.

With two members of the planned rescue team, that left Hadrian for Eric to prod along toward a quicker mission start.

Belly full of pancakes, Eric made his way through the ship and to the quarters where Hadrian and Sparta lived. He gave a quick, polite knock on the door.

"Busy. Go away."

A "busy, go away" from Uncle Enzio was usually enough to get rid of Eric for hours. But Hadrian wasn't Uncle Enzio anymore. And Eric wasn't really Eric anymore, either.

This Eric, wearing his official *Arete* wizard uniform (with a light smudge of pancake syrup), would not be cowed so easily. He did not go away. He waited.

Never great with chronos, even before studying magic, he'd learned the lengths of a number of songs. A silent karaoke session broke out in the wizard's head; his own voice plus the music from the omni.

Cabin Bop, by Jacie and the Moonshadows

Spin, Spin, Spin, by Orbital Station: Funk

The club remix of Galonica's *Five is Right*

Reflection of my Heartbeat, by Mindy Mun

No outside observer would have overheard a single note or sung lyric, but they'd definitely have recognized the telltale elbow shimmies and hip wiggles of a guy with a song stuck in his head.

Just before launching into Handstand Frown's classic, *Love Thy Enemy,* he decided to knock again.

"Have you been standing out there this whole damned time?"

"Yes," Eric admitted loudly enough to be heard through the door.

Stomping bare footsteps preceded the opening of the door —by scientific gizmo, so Hadrian couldn't have been *that* mad. "What? What's so blasted important?"

The younger/older wizard wore nothing but a bathrobe cinched at the waist. He was sweaty, with rumpled hair and his face flushed. A glance past him showed Sparta lounging on the bed in similar disarray and clad in—as near Eric could tell—a thin satin sheet.

"Oh. Were you just... I mean..."

"Yes," Hadrian replied with a scowl.

"Um. Sorry. I mean..."

"Eric..."

"It's a matter of life and death!" he blurted.

Rather than transform at the news, Hadrian's ire only hardened. "Interrupting my quietude has often carried those stakes."

Sparta climbed out of bed, clutching the sheets to her collarbone and giving what looked to be a practiced twirl as her feet touched the floor, turning the bedding into a makeshift wrap gown. "Eric, have you, by any remote chance, been attempting to tamper with the timeline in an effort to prevent your father's capture?"

Eric blinked in shock. "No! That would be preposterous."

"You're lying," Hadrian told him.

"No... it's just..."

"You're evading," Hadrian clarified. "It's a type of lying at which your father excels and one at which you are hopeless. Out with it. What have you done?"

"*Other* than damn near split my head like firewood," Sparta added.

"I did what? I'm so, *so* sorry if your oracleyness got hurt seeing or hearing things, but... you... look OK. Are you OK now?"

"I'm holding her magic in check. Should do the same for you, except you're squirrely as wet soap and more bother than it's worth if you can be trusted to manage your own business. Which, clearly, you can't."

Every puff of air was squeezed out of Eric's lungs just then —metaphorically, anyway. He could breathe just fine, but his magic was suddenly a bug in a jam jar with no air holes.

"Wait. Stop. I need to talk to you."

"You're talking already. Keep going."

"OK. So... Dad died."

"He WHAT! Those rotten eyndar will RUE the day they—"

"Not yet!" Eric interjected. "In about two days. You and Jessie get there too late. What I'm trying to say is, just hurry her along and maybe you get to Dad in time."

"*How* do you know this?" Hadrian's words dripped menace.

It was slowly creeping back into Eric's mind just what Mordecai The Brown had been known for prior to becoming an outlaw with Dad. He'd hunted down dark wizards for a living and, to hear him tell it, for fun. The Brown family was fabulously rich; he didn't need the money from what was a reasonably well-paid job. He liked doling out his brand of justice to those he deemed to deserve it.

Eric cringed and cowered and tried to look small. Even with shoes on and Hadrian barefoot, the taller wizard made that part easy for him. "I... I... worried that this might go badly and set up a recursive time loop so that if Dad dies I get to try again to save him."

"You used chronomancy."

Eric gave a chihuahua's nod.

"How many times?"

"Pardon?"

"How many times have we been through this loop of yours?" Hadrian turned to Sparta. "Could this explain your episode just now?"

She shook her head, jangling a million terras' worth of jewelry. "I don't know. I've never experienced anything like it before. Maybe. Best I can give you is a maybe. Is there any way to break a time loop?"

"Can you see anything helpful?" Eric inquired.

"No," Hadrian snapped. "She sees a mind-searing chaos that I'm presently protecting her from. And you haven't answered me. How many times has this loop reset?"

Suddenly, Eric wasn't sure of the answer. "The first one. I think. But... it's possible it's just the first time I remember. As for breaking the loop, we have to get Dad out of the Eyndar Empire alive. If you leave now, you can probably—"

"That's *one* way to break the loop. If the loop is inexpertly constructed, killing the originator would do the trick."

Eric took a step back. "You're... not serious..."

Hadrian's eyes were so much older than the rest of him. Eric had to avert his own. Hadrian's voice was calm with menace. "Let's think this through. If we're in a primary loop, and Sparta suffered that attack, then additional loops might grow progressively worse. You might even kill her."

"But I—"

"Then again, maybe that's how it goes *every* time, and this is the umpteenth iteration of your time-travel hell prison, and you can't get it to resolve. Fundamental flaw. Conflict with Fate itself. Who knows. If you're forgetting multiple loops, then saving Carl is either damn near impossible or doesn't end the loop. We may have had this conversation every time. Normally, I'd give you leeway, try to help you through a successful rescue attempt."

"Right. We should round up Jessie and—"

"She's not ready. Maybe she doesn't need to be, but I need to think this through. If I go with my inclination, we'll likely follow through on a plan similar to other multi-loop plans that have failed already."

"Maybe..." Eric allowed. He wasn't liking how this was going.

"To escape a loop, we need to go against our instincts. Especially if you don't remember the loops and aren't making informed decisions about changes. On the other hand, if this *is* the initial loop after the first reset, then Sparta's on the chopping block as future iterations would presumably compound her visions. Need to nip this in the bud."

"Right. Good. So, let's find Jessie. We can launch right away."

"This mission was always a long shot. I don't mind risking my life for Carl. He's always done the same. But you... you little ingrate. I loved a woman for sixty years, and I put aside thoughts of chronomancy to save her. If this works, I'll have a hell of a lot of explaining to do. But better men have done worse in service of a greater good. And if it doesn't work... well, you'll know how badly you fucked up."

"I *KNOW* how much I fucked up," Eric protested, frustrated doubly for how thoroughly Hadrian was clamping his magic down.

"Not yet, you don't."

Suddenly, there was a crunchy crackle. The hallway spun around him, and Eric was facing the wall across from Hadrian and Sparta's room instead of looking into it.

"Now, you understand."

Eric tried to answer, but instead...

A fork fell with a clatter that rang through the dining lounge.

IT ALL STARTS HERE

———

That big MEANIE.

Hadrian had killed him.

This was the dining lounge.

These were Eric's strawberry pancakes with butter and syrup.

Dad was alive, but a moment ago, Eric hadn't been.

Suddenly, despite a delicious plate in front of him, Eric wasn't hungry.

How many times had Uncle Enzio been ready to kill him if Eric had taken a step too far? And the ease with which he'd done it. Against Aunt Tiffany, Eric had felt like he was fighting for control of his magic, mumbling at the universe with her hand covering his mouth. Hadrian had buried him alive for all that anyone could hear him shouting.

OK. Time had reset. The loop magic had worked. Clearly, without Eric's intervention, Dad had died again, and since Eric wasn't alive for the two days, to him it had felt like nothing. He hoped Hadrian had felt *really* guilty the whole time. Frankly, if Jessie had still agreed to go on a mission with him, Eric would have been shocked.

Then again, Hadrian had probably vaporized him. In the swirl of activity planning the rescue, it was conceivable that no one had noticed him missing... No. That wasn't possible. Charlotte would have intervened. They'd have launched a search. Sparta would have had to lie and maybe get caught and...

None of these thoughts were useful.

That was a Charlotte-ism. She'd taught him how to catch a thought spiral before it built too much momentum.

Eric simply took the knowledge that Hadrian would kill him for creating this time loop, folded it up, and tucked it in an envelope in the back of his mind.

OK. Eric would no longer attempt to involve Hadrian directly in the recovery plan.

This time around, Eric hadn't spooked Jessie yet, so he had another shot at getting to her and making a difference that way.

"What?" she demanded when the door opened. "You know I'm busy." She wagged a datapad in case he didn't know what busy was supposed to look like.

He didn't need to see the screen to know that it was July 20, 2592.

"You know that talk Mom had with us about procrastination?"

"This is a mission to save Dad, not some bullshit school assignment or a free clinic appointment."

Eric had almost forgotten that period when Mom had begun refusing to schedule Jessie for medical checkups and made her do it herself. Actually, it was right around the time that Eric had started seeing Convocation healers because he kept fouling up hand scanners. Free clinics stopped being free around the time you broke their toys.

"Right. All the more reason to hit the unfriendly vacuum and grab Dad from the eyndar."

Jessie set side the datapad and put both hands on Eric's shoulders. "Eric, I love you. I know you mean well. We're keeping close tabs on the newsfeeds. They've got him on there daily now. There's a list kilometers long of eyndar citizens who want to give him a piece of their mind. If ever there was a guy built to take verbal abuse and come out just fine, it's Dad. I know you don't understand graphs, but there's one zig-zaggy line going up which is operational readiness and another going steadily down with time until the eyndar start killing Dad every day."

"Right. I know. It's just that..."

"We'll be ready to go before he's in real, immediate danger. But we also want the best chance of success. And if that means a few hundred more aggrieved assholes get to scream at Dad—"

"Wasn't that your band?"

"Huh?" Jessie blinked. "No. That was Aggrieved Asshats. And how come you even remember that?"

"I went to all your shows."

"There were two. We sucked. And the music store recovered all the gear we stole. Why can you remember stupid bullshit from when we were kids but not how to follow a chain of command? You work for Hadrian now. Go bother him."

"But—"

The door slid shut in Eric's face.

———

Several minutes later, in a far-off section of the *Arete*, another door opened.

"Hey, Eric. What's up?" Trebla asked, stepping aside and implicitly inviting him inside.

His laaku cousin's quarters were always such a place of wonder and mystery. Of all the crew—with the exception of Grosstet—he'd done the most to make his quarters homey. And more than anyone else, including the haathee, he'd made use of the vertical space. Hooks welded to the ceiling dangled innumerable ropes and cables that supported furniture, artwork, snack sacks, and storage bins. A swinging lounger couch at head height, accessible via rope-and-bar steps, offered a premium view of the holo-projector. The hot tub had a slide at one end and a drink bar at the other. A woven leather hammock swung in the breeze of a warm air current from the life support vents.

"You're still listening to Stale Can again?" Eric asked, recognizing the ambient music filling the room.

Trebla ambled over to the coffee machine, perched on one of the few structures fixed to the floor. "Jazzi got me back onto the tram with a lot of old stuff. She doesn't have pics, obviously, but back on Phabian, she kept her hair short and styled it into fur spikes. Green tint, if you can believe it."

"I can. Where is Jasmine, anyway?" Eric made a show of looking around, but other than behind the opening to the washroom, there was no likely place for her to be hiding.

"Early shift. Her boss is kind of an asshole, but he's gotta be if he doesn't want to crash this luxury starliner he's piloting these days. Interest you in a cup?" Trebla poured a second coffee and offered it.

Eric immediately searched out the local sugar supply. "Thanks."

"So, what brings you by?"

"Uh. Just wanted to see how you were coming along with plans to rescue Dad."

Trebla chuckled and sipped his coffee. "I'm gonna let you in on a little secret. Also the reason you never win at poker night. Whenever you've got an ulterior motive or are trying to think up a lie, you start with 'uh.' And you hardly ever do it otherwise."

"I do?"

"You do."

"Darn."

"Wanna try again? Why'd you really stop by?"

Eric was a fast learner. He wasn't going to get caught in the trap Trebla had *just* pointed out. He concentrated hard on not hemming or hawing when he next spoke. "Dad died in a couple days and I set it up so I'm trapped in a perpetual time loop until I can figure out a way to save him. I'm hoping I can just rush things along a bit so Jessie and Hadrian can get there in time."

Trebla drained his coffee. "Well... that's what I get, I guess, for giving away your tell."

He hadn't really *meant* to just blurt all that out. It just happened to be the best way to ensure he wasn't going to stumble over his words when they came out. But admitting all that and still not having Trebla believe him...

An idea poofed to the fore of Eric's mind. "OK, smarty-hands. Think of a password. Something I won't guess."

"Eric, you're an idiot."

"I'd definitely guess that in three tries."

"No. I mean you're being an idiot. Everyone said you couldn't go back in time, even when they said it was possible but super stupid to go forward. It's supposed to blow up the universe or some shit."

"It didn't."

"My point, exactly. What's more likely: that you traveled back in time a couple days or conjured up a vision of the coming couple days so vivid that you fooled yourself?"

Eric blinked.

His mind took a brief sabbatical.

The alert sound of Trebla's datapad snapped Eric back to his senses.

"Yo!" Trebla answered with a smile on his face that could only mean one person on the other end.

"*Hey, you still loafing around back home?*" Jasmine asked.

"Yeah, I am, but—"

"*Great. Stay there. Got the pulse transmission fluid swapped on Line 97 ahead of schedule. Plenty of spare fluid, and Grosstet was adamant that the stuff is perfectly biosafe. I was thinking we can try that lemon juicer and—*"

That was the point at which Trebla managed to get a word in edgewise. "Eric's here."

"*Oh. Hi, Eric. Can I get Trebla to myself for like... what do you think you're good for, schnook'ems? Eight minutes? Ten? No rush. It'll take me five just getting back there.*"

"I... uh... sure thing."

"Catch you when you crash, babe," Trebla replied before shutting off the comm. He aimed a finger from one lower hand at Eric. "Finish that coffee, and you're outta here."

Eric's eyes slowly scanned the countertop where the coffee maker resided. "You... hmm... how to put this... don't seem to have a lemon juicer."

"Yeah. Uh-huh." Trebla placed one hand on Eric's back, gently guiding him toward the door, and retrieved the coffee cup with another.

"And last I heard, we don't have lemons on board." Eric liked to know when new and interesting foods came aboard the *Arete*. He got regular updates from Falgapap when, for instance, pancake-grade strawberries arrived.

"Fairy-tale time is over, pal," Trebla informed him as Eric was prodded out the door. "You wanna play time-travel hero, go find your own girl."

That was a great idea.

Except Charlotte was on duty, and he didn't need to get kicked off the bridge.

⊐⊏

The rest of the workday, Eric wandered the *Arete*, getting quite an education about what everyone actually spent their time on. It frankly amazed him how long simple tasks like cooking meals, reorganizing the hangar, and tightening loose spaceships took. By their own accounts, most of these people were *good* at their jobs.

Lisa insisted that hosting the self-defense classes was still a valuable use of her time since the brain couldn't go on working indefinitely without mixing in some exercise. This was news to Eric.

Tippitak talked him through the process of arranging

supply drops by digital banking trickery and scheduling deep space dead drops for pickups. Eric learned that this was where his strawberries came from. He'd always assumed a farm of some sort.

Before chasing him out of Med Bay on safety-of-her-H-tech-stuff grounds, Harmony had been gogglesing at very small things that didn't look sick to Eric.

Mindy and Daphne had turned the study of Earth-like eyndar homeworld maps into a couples' activity. They'd taken one of the many spare haathee lounges as a workstation, using datapads and a portable holo-projector above table height while playing with one another's bare feet below. Maybe it was xenoist of him, but Eric was glad that Charlotte wasn't fuzzy. In fact, Eric *knew* that humans grew more hair than what Charlotte sported, but she was smooth and pleasant to the touch basically all over.

By the time Eric was done absorbing the anthropo-geographic differences between the eyndar homeworld and Denmark, Eric was in the mood for a different kind of Danish.

The dining lounge didn't have anything like a Danish on hand, so Eric hung around the saloon.

Figgy did nothing all day. It was something the two of them had in common. But now that Eric had an Important Mission He Couldn't Reveal, it cast their situations in stark contrast. Eric was always supposed to be at the ready. Hadrian might have taken his job, but Eric had always been an on-call sort of wizard, ready to jump from sessile to essential at a moment's notice. Abandoned pancakes and half-eaten Snakki Bars attested to his ever-ready status.

But Figgy was simply lazy.

"Can I pose you a hypothetical?" Eric asked.

Figarus of Alspen breathed out a cloud of hashish smoke

from the hookah lounge's central supply. "In pondering that question, I believe you already have."

That was as close to a straight answer as Eric was liable to get. "Fine. Well, here's another. Imagine we are trapped in a time loop."

"We are."

Eric wasn't prepared for this level of acceptance of his premise.

"We are, because time *is* a loop, my friend. Beginning to end. End to beginning. Old philosophers used to have patience for it; they'd meet themselves over and over, simply by waiting. Time just got too big, man. Too big. Ain't nobody got time for that kind of waiting anymore."

This was the point at which Eric realized Figgy wasn't going to be any help at all. If he was going to get anything useful from the laaku philosopher, it would either have to wait until tomorrow or a subsequent loop.

Eric wasn't being a pessimist here. He was just coming to the realization that this was nearly the end of Day One of a two-day reprieve, and he wasn't feeling like he was making any progress at all toward altering history.

Sure, maybe he hadn't eaten a saloon Danish for dinner the first time through, and he hadn't been alive by dinnertime the second. By his best estimation, this was his third loop, and mealtimes weren't a likely source of meaningful changes.

He made sure to be home in his quarters by the time Charlotte arrived.

She entered in her therapist attire. Long skirt. High heels, which she shed immediately upon crossing the threshold. Fluffy sweater, which she deposited over the back of a chair on her way past, revealing a black button-down blouse underneath.

"How was everything?" Eric inquired cheerily.

Charlotte sighed elaborately and draped her wrists over Eric's shoulders, lacing delicate fingers at the back of his neck. For his part, Eric held her by the waist. "Once Hadrian made clear that he was capable of consulting on the magic without support, I've been largely left to run the ship as I see fit."

Eric silently noted that "as she saw fit" didn't seem to involve him any more than "how Jessie saw fit," since this was the first he'd heard of it. "Interesting patients? Juicy gossip?" *Anything that might materially affect tomorrow's mission to save Dad?,* he silently added.

They moved the conversation to the couch, where Charlotte lay with her head in Eric's lap and her feet over the arm. "Oh, let's see... what's harmless enough to share?"

Eric slipped the cosmetic spectacles off her face and allowed the wire rims with their flimsy arms and optically inert lenses to float nearby. He brushed a lock of stray hair from her eyes and combed his fingers through the rest, fingertips massaging Charlotte's scalp and drawing a contented little moan.

"Well, for starters, Tippitak is pregnant again."

Ooh, this was juicy. If he got nothing else from this loop, Eric was going to chalk up at least a minor win. He hadn't gleaned this tidbit his first time around. "Is Makket the father?"

Charlotte gently rocked her head back and forth. "She isn't sure. Hasn't spoken to Dr. Richelieu yet about it. Apparently, science can tell if it cares to get nosy. Apples to carrots, Oracle Sparta could unravel the mystery with a glance."

"Might not want to bother her," Eric stated emphatically. "I hear she's under a bit of unnatural weather. Something about her visions being too much."

"Imagine... this place being more interesting to the future than the whole of Oxford. Did I mention remembering her from school?"

"No." Eric was fairly certain he'd never known that.

"Delved my memories a smidge. Saw her about campus here and there. All those wizards with all those myriad futures ahead of them—myself included—and this motley assortment of chocolate-coated miscreants finally pushes her past her limits to block out?"

Charlotte had already eaten while on duty and Eric had been grazing on junk food throughout the day, suspecting there would be no consequences to doing so. After a few routine preparations and the extinguishing of the room's science lights, the pair crawled beneath the covers and snuggled up together.

"Where shall we venture?"

Eric paused a moment. This was going to be tricky. They were already inside a time loop. The Village of Eternity existed; he could tell even while awake. But venturing inside could prove legitimately dangerous. What might happen if the loop reset while he was outside the standard curvature of time? Could he emerge in the dining hall with time racing past him or so slow he could barely interact with his surroundings? He could reset it still stuck inside the Village of Eternity with no body outside to return to.

And there was always that complete unraveling of space and time that everyone kept yakking about.

"I... don't think I can tonight."

"Oh? What's wrong?"

The best truths were half-truths. "It's the whole thing with Dad. I just..." He trailed off, unsure how to proceed.

A soft finger came to rest across his lips. "Say no more. Our adventures are a treat. An escape. But lifetimes filled with worry about an uncertain future are no reward. Take a break from those cares. We'll continue our outings from reality once your father is safe."

"You mean it?" This was going much easier than he expected.

"I spent half the day dealing with people who deny they have inner turmoil and the remainder seeing those same people awash in confusion and despair over the simplest of emotional conundrums. Someone taking an active role in mental self-care is, to be frank, refreshing."

"You're so sweet."

"Well, no need to gush about it. You don't owe me centuries of entertainment at your own expense. However, I suggest we rearrange ourselves oppositely. Wrap one arm about me and use my pectoral muscle for a pillow for once."

"But, that would—" He caught himself. Of course, Charlotte knew anatomy better than he did.

The pair squooshed and rubbed and slithered together until both seemed satisfied that they could fall toward slumber without cricks in necks or limbs losing circulation.

Eric drifted off to sleep listening to Charlotte's steady heartbeat.

⸺

The following morning, Trebla was at work in his lab. Yesterday's trials had gone well, but he'd been using stand-alone plates to test the concept. Beneath his scope, he viewed the black leather tactical gloves in stereoscopic magnification. He had calculated a perfect spread pattern for the tetra-acetate haathee adhesive gel for full coverage, uniform thickness under compression, and minimum curing time.

Unfortunately, the simulations hadn't taken into account the pain-in-the-ass process of squirting that pattern out of a nozzle smaller than a water-flosser.

Trebla's fingers shook like he was verging on hypothermia,

but that was mainly thanks to the magnification. The micro-thin layering he had planned all boiled down to exacting minutiae. Emphasis on the "minute."

The door opened, and Trebla jerked. A thick, gloppy squiggle raced across the intricate maze of epoxy lines he'd sketched out.

"FUCK!"

"Oopsie doopsie," Jomek called out merrily as he entered bearing two giant mugs. "Told ya. Program a printing arm. Be quicker that way." He extended one as a peace offering. Dark roast from the hidden engineering stash, by the aroma.

"Thanks," Trebla griped, snatching one away but reserving judgment on an actual apology.

"You see Eric? Got me on the way here. Much yakkity; many yak."

Trebla grunted. "Yeah. Could say I saw him. Stopped by a few minutes ago. Never heard so many tech questions out of him. Why yes, Eric, the adhesive really *is* very sticky. Yes, this is spare hull plating we found in the hangar. No, Eric, it doesn't come in other colors."

"Not very technical."

"For Eric?"

"Gotcha gotcha. Point taken. How long you think you gonna be? I still think a big 'ole glop in the middle and wipe the edge after you smoosh, gonna be fine."

Trebla sighed. Jomek wasn't going to convince him to slap a trowel of adhesive on the back of the gloves like he was laying bricks, but he was probably right that having a machine do the application would be faster, even accounting for programming time. Messing up and starting from scratch after cleaning and prepping the surface again was a kick in the junk every time.

"Hey. You know the guy better, eh?" Jomek asked casually. "He off orbit from usual?"

"He's never been orbital as long as I've known him."

Jomek shook his head. "Nah. Elliptical's still an orbit. But Eric doesn't seem right compared to himself. Asking me all sorts of things about Shuttle 1 and who flies best and—"

Trebla knew what the guy meant. "He was trying to rush me. I figured he was just antsy about Uncle Carl—who isn't?—but you think maybe he's angling to take a crack at making the rescue himself?"

Jomek laid a hand on Trebla's shoulder. "I could tell you 'no' if it would make you work better."

A glance at the freshly cleaned glove, glistening with fast-evap astringent solution, stared up at him accusingly.

"Just in case, go swap the access code on Shuttle 1. Grosstet would be able to override it, but nobody else. Only tell me and Jessie the new code."

Jomek nodded. "Good call. I go. You... fix those gloves up right. Don't want the captain getting shot because you got lazy."

———

Britney squeezed one eye shut and peered into the open mouth of Konoha, who sat with his little boots dangling over the edge of the table in Exam Room 3. While her goggles could take care of the magnification, keeping both eyes open just didn't feel like it helped.

"Well, the good news is, you broke your top two incisors above the gumline."

"Im-whuff-way-iv-vhat-goob-nooz?-I-um-im-confibrable-paim-aw-fhanks-do-vhat-wiffle-bafterd-mephew-uv-mime."

The analgesic spray injector was set to basic human. Too low a dose for her, based on mass alone, but ludicrous overkill for Konoha. The ratatoret wouldn't feel most of his body if she gave him that much. Tap-tap-tapping down until she had a more suitable dosage, she pantomimed with finger and thumb.

"Open up. This'll fix the sting."

"Aaaaaaaaaaaaaaah."

The vocal accompaniment wasn't necessary, but Britney didn't object. A hiss-puff in the upper jaw, and within seconds, the ratatoret's posture relaxed.

"Muff-bebber-Fanku-Mebic-Bwitney."

"Just hang in there. We'll bond in some ceramite extensions. I've got dimensions from your previous scans. You'll need to come in every so often to get them trimmed down since the ceramite won't wear like normal teeth."

Konoha huffed a little sigh. "I-kem-embure-vhe-imcomvemiemthe-of-fweqwemt-Meb-Bay-vithith-if-ib-meamth-I-dom'p-hab-oo-thubthitht-om-peamud-bubber."

"You don't have to worry," Britney assured him. "We'll make sure that eating peamud bubber is a choice, not a medical necessity."

The little Logistics support worker shot her a dirty glare, but Britney had timed her teasing for just after she'd clamped the custom mold in place and was injecting the ceramite resin.

"Hi, you busy?"

Britney turned to find Wizard Eric behind her. She shot him a scowl and tried to hide the fact that she found him scary. Sure, she could throw him over a shoulder and carry him to the lift without breaking a sweat or straining a muscle. But by the same token, he could turn her bones to pudding or disconnect her from the concept of gravity.

"You don't look sick. Or hurt. You know Dr. Richelieu's rules."

"I know, I know," Wizard Eric mollified her. "But today is sort of a consequences-lite day. Do you mind if I ask you a number of questions of a highly personal nature related to someone who isn't me?"

"Um. Yes," Britney replied. "That's unethical. If you want to know someone's personal medical information, ask them yourself. If they say 'no,' there's your answer." She turned to her little patient. The curing cycle had finished. She removed the mold. "You're good, soldier. Back to the front lines with you. And don't bite any more aluminum peanuts."

"Thank-you-Medic-Britney-I'm-feeling-better-already-I-hope-to-take-your-advice-and-not-return-for-a-similar-accident-in-the-future."

"Day after tomorrow... we'll file that ceramite down."

"Kibbibon again?" Wizard Eric asked. The ratatoret replied only with a rueful nod. Once Konoha was gone, he shut his eyes and muttered, "Konoha. Aluminum peanut. Broken teeth."

"You're still here," Britney pointed out. "Am I going to have to get Dr. Richelieu?"

"It's about Jessie," the wizard blurted. "And I'm willing to make a deal."

"Deal? What deal? What do you think this is, a swap meet? I'm not making any deals."

"But... what if I could get you something you desperately want?" Wizard Eric teased.

A chill ran up Britney's spine. She really had to stop watching those horror holos. This was either the devil himself in human guise, or this floppy little twig of a wizard had similar tastes in entertainment. Nevertheless, the question was designed to be irresistible.

"How would you even know what I want?"

"You'd have to tell me. But I'm a pretty resourceful guy when I have to be."

Britney gulped. She wasn't qualified for this. On the *Scylla*, the ssentuadi kept mostly to themselves. They didn't slither around the ship making cryptic offers and wheedling for deals.

"I... I wouldn't know where to start. Some other time, maybe."

"There won't *be* other times," the wizard insisted. "And I'm not asking a lot. I'm probably willing to offer a whole lot more."

"What *are* you asking about? Enough all-round-the-mulberry-bush with you. Just spit it out."

Wizard Eric tucked his hands into his sleeves and huffed. "I want to know what's wrong with Jessie that has Harmony worried about her going on this mission."

Britney cast the wizard a wary look. "That's all?" In the grand scheme, it didn't sound so bad. Dr. Richelieu would be off her head if someone could convince Captain Ramsey to send someone else on that crazy rescue mission.

"That's all. In return... hmm... how about I tell you everything I know about Harmony? I've known her most of my life. We've never been... like... close-close... but I bet I have plenty of dirt that you could use for... whatever. Whether you want to be a better assistant. Whether you want to make friends. If you want to kiss up to the boss. Or... if 'up to' isn't really what you were hoping."

It took a second for the nonsense to unravel, and Britney felt her cheeks warm.

She swallowed. "It's not... it's not like that..."

"Not my business," the captain's little brother replied. "Just information. Do what you like with it. Shape a relationship or just tuck it away in a little box to enjoy knowing. I just want to know what's wrong with my sister."

Britney found herself nodding. What could be the harm? Kid was just worried about his sister.

As for Dr. Richelieu... she wouldn't mind getting to know the doctor a little better.

Lisa's chopsticks dove into her ramen and came up with long strands of noodles. Across from her, Eric ate a similar bowl, minus the pork and egg. Had been nice noshing on a good egg, now and then, with Chik-ta off in Hidden-Repair-Base-Land with Junior. Could've done with the vacation herself, but she didn't envy the dirty looks from that egg-minder any time she was trying to have a decent breakfast—or, in this case, lunch.

"Been hearing that Jessie's halfway to almost being nearly considered something of a bit of a wizard," Eric remarked offhandedly. Pointedly offhandedly, if that were a thing. Almost drawing absurd amounts of attention to his own innocuousness.

"Out with it, lad," Lisa cajoled him. "What's it you're on about? I got ten things between now and dinner, and you ain't makin' it eleven without a tussle."

"Oh. Nothing. Just making conversation. Hadrian's been teaching her, and I just wanted to know what your thoughts were."

"Piece of work, ain't she, that sister of yours? Harm does her up with some fancy elephant techno, and she up and decides to go goofy on us. No offense."

"None taken," Eric assured her. Well, all right then.

"Thing is, as kids, that Uncle Enzio of yours put it pretty clear. Any of us kiddos wanted tutelage in the dark arts, he'd be more than obliged. Mum and Dad, they didn't have to worry none. We was hardly around much, and flyin' was loads better'n party tricks with floatin' cans and what-have-you. None of you *Mobius* brats had the first inkling, so why should we; yourself bein' the exception, naturally."

"Naturally."

"Jess was one of us. Reserve corps, o' course. Nagged after us to play pilotin' games when me and Junior was learnin' on the McCoy. Ozzy and the laaku kiddos, they didn't show so much as a glimmer. Now... Jess's gone and turned her coat, tugged out her sleeves, and now she's decided she's magical?"

"She's really not. It's just... like kung fu."

"Like in the holos. Yeah. I seen her. Peeked in on the gym when she's by herself o' late. Flippin' and flyin' like some damned character. Not a real person."

"Like Aunt Tiffany?" Eric suggested.

Lisa grunted through a mouthful of noodles before swallowing. "Nah. Tiffany's got a sort of... don't know how to put it. She could tear the skin off'n ya like old wallpaper, but she wouldn't make it look like trouble. Jess is all lookin' like she's chuggin' blaster plasma."

"You don't think it's a good look?"

"A good look? Fuck me, ask Junior. He's the one what had his hand in the cookies. Soz. Sister and all. Don't mean nothing. Just... is it me or is it bonkers to put two wizards in a shuttle and pack 'em off to save yer dad? One's wet behind the ears and green as moss. The other's learned three chords and fixing to play Wembley."

Eric's empty bowl slid aside with his chopstick lying across the rim and not a finger touching it. "How could you see it going wrong? No one listens to me, so you can admit anything."

What was the harm? He had ears and he had a point. Nobody paid a lick of attention to what Eric Ramsey had to say. Not when it came to being wrong about quoting old songs. Not when it came to ghosts and goblins in the canyons outside Carson Colony. He was so habitually wrong that Lisa could have made a fortune dragging him to the roulette tables in Vegas Prime and betting against him.

"Lemme tell yous, a million and one damn things nobody will say a peep about when it comes to this bloody tram wreck of a mission. First, I—"

Lisa's TeleJack hummed.

"Shite."

"Problem?" the wizard asked, trying and failing to sound nonchalant.

She twisted her wrist to show him.

Security alert. Intruder in engineering lab. This is a drill.

"But if it's a—"

"A drill? A test? Don't matter, boy-o. Gots to get a move on."

Lisa raced from the dining lounge, hoping to grab a weapon before she made it to the engineering lab to find out what the fuck Jess was up to.

Eric knew where this was all headed. He had been there before. Trebla was making the weird gloves. Lisa was running off to help test them. If Eric wanted to stay ahead of the game, he needed to get into position early and make himself scarce.

The Briefing Room was a place Eric visited more often than he was invited. The former was rarely, the latter was never these days. Charlotte had been tapped to arrange the magical oversight of Dad's rescue. And once Hadrian had tossed his hat into the ring (proverbially, Eric presumed), he'd all but ousted her.

It was hard to argue with a wizard in general, Uncle Enzio especially, and if Hadrian was on the verge of outright admitting he was Mordecai The Brown, the odds of anyone getting a word in against him without permission seemed remote.

The overly large haathee table had been lowered to a height more manageable for the majority of the *Arete's* crew, but the length and width still hinted that maybe half a herd of elephants could congregate around it socially. Unlike many a human-made conference table, there was room beneath it to huddle with little fear of knees and kicking feet. Plus, based on the accommodations, he knew where Makket and Trebla would be seated side by side, allowing even more room.

Cloaking himself in invisibility, Eric huddled under the table and waited.

His bowl of ramen grumbled in his tummy.

It had only been around half past noon, and unless he'd altered the timeline more than he'd imagined, Jessie was going to call for a final briefing at three.

Crawling back out from under the table, Eric slunk off, found a washroom, relaxed as best he was able with his mind in an absolute tizzy, and returned somewhere around two thirty.

Shortly before three, the attendees started attending.

Eric had been here the first time, so he listened carefully to try and determine whether his actions had made any changes in the plan or even the meeting itself.

Lisa was in charge of presenting. A hum from the table above him hinted that someone had turned on the holo-projector.

"This is the Eyndar Empire homeworld. Earth-like in name only. Rotten doggos gone and wrecked it up something awful. Capital city, Imand'Vol, is roundabout where Copenhagen Prime oughtta be." So far, so same. "This here mess is what they call a city. An' I don't want a word out of you wizzies that it ain't no worse than Earth. It is."

Sounded rehearsed. Lisa probably had a script memorized, or at least some ad-libbing that nothing had derailed.

"The other shite I got in red here is the imperial palace, the military headquarters, and the clubhouse of their take on a Convocation."

Hadrian harrumphed softly. "Least of our worries. Those

tail-chasing moon-magi outsource their real magic, and their Luna isn't even in phase right now."

All right. This was getting somewhere. Hadrian was different. Well, maybe not fundamentally, but he was alterable in the timeline. Or maybe the timeline was more mutable for him. Either way, he was Eric's first glimmer of hope for an alternative outcome.

"Gonna start with the good news," Lisa continued. "This here's a festival in the middle of summer. Gonna be loads of strangers in town, loaded up in cool-suits and breather masks. Most of the locals can take the air quality bein' 750 parts per million. Special injections and implants and whatnot. Offworld visitors, not so much. We got a pair of cool-suits and snout-masks with goggles to keep the doggos from catchin' on right off."

Eric had worn one of those getups—or something close, anyway—as a Halloween costume one year. Dad had insisted that Eric was scary, and until just now, Eric hadn't considered believing him.

"That ends the good news. Now for the bad. You lot are going to perform a blind suborbital, subterranean astral drop from the nosebleed astral straight down this here sewer main. Assuming you survive, on account of the rest of this plan don't do a whole lot if you push daisies halfway to getting there, you'll head out through the cleansing station and across a couple streets to the prison. Ain't no direct route in pipes on account of the doggos is too dumb to rebuild a thousand-year-old-prison with modern plumbing. You'll sneak as far into the prison as you can get, then you fight the rest of the way, grab Carl, and skedaddle back out. Easy peasy."

There were a few nervous laughs around the briefing table.

"Not a laughing matter," Hadrian pointed out. "The hard

part will be getting to Carl before those eyndar get the yips. I lay eyes on him, it's clear sailing through bloody waters."

No. No. NO. This was the same as before. Why? Why, Hadrian? Couldn't you come up with some new ideas?

The meeting wrapped up. It was all double-checking stuff he'd been hearing since the planning began, anyway. Feet and hands and fluffy little tails made their way from the Briefing Room in an orderly shuffle.

Jessie waited for them. Charlotte lingered. Just like before.

Please be different. Please be different.

"A word, before you depart?"

"Go ahead. You're as good as in command already."

So far, so same. Darn it!

"It's about your brother." Still an odd way to refer to him in front of Jessie. Couldn't she just call him Eric?

"You handle him better than I do, these days. What's the problem with him?"

"He's been acting strangely."

Jessie laughed. Not even her fun, break-the-tension laugh, but a mocking one that rankled her brother. "Please tell me this isn't the first time you noticed."

"Strangely given his baseline idiosyncrasies. Just the past two days or so. He's squirreling all over the ship, bothering everyone about odd details of their involvement in the rescue efforts."

Eric scowled. Last time through, that accusation hadn't made much sense. He'd gone about his usual business, he thought.

"Yeah, people have been coming to me, too," Jessie admitted. Eric breathed a sigh of relief. He *had* been more bothersome this time through. Good. He hadn't given this timeline much of a nudge, but maybe he could start it rocking, like a playground swing or a canoe where everyone was yelling for him to sit down and he would just as soon as the silly thing held still long enough.

"I worry he might try stowing away. I haven't seen him in hours, and I was looking."

"Try Sparta?"

A cold metaphoric wind blew through the Briefing Room. "No. I shan't. I merely suggest that Hadrian might give Shuttle 1 a once-over before departure."

"Will do."

There was no protest this time. No insistence that Eric wouldn't be stupid enough to try that. Paradoxically, he wondered if that was the universe telling him he ought to try.

Not this time, however. Not with them alert and on guard. Time loops were puzzles to solve. And since he'd already ventured into at least a third loop by now, counting the abbreviated encounter with Hadrian's cold-blooded temper, this was clearly more than a simple chance for a do-over.

Eric waited until the two most important people in his life drifted off, then counted to a thousand, then slunk out of the Briefing Room to return to visibility in the nearest washroom.

———

In a prison in the bowels of the nameless hole where eyndar buried their prisoners before turning them to bones, Carl Ramsey struck up a conversation with the guard who entered.

"Look who's next in line to piss on the human," he called out.

"Shut up, f-f-f-filth."

Carl grinned despite himself. "Hey, one of you f-f-f-fuckers learned to speak English. Just f-f-f-fair warning, pal, I've started giving out ratings. And since I promised him, and I don't go back on my word, your associate Gelnatra is hung like a stick of lip tint that someone rolled in honey and loose azrin fur. Rest assured, everyone who comes after you will hear about your equipment."

The guard switched back to his own language. "What part of 'shut up' didn't you grasp, human?"

"The 'up,' I guess. Never really did make sense. Shut? Sure. Mouth open; you want it closed. That's the verb for you. But when you add the 'up,' who are you even talking to, now? My lower jaw? Lower lip? Am I supposed to maybe throw my head back?"

The eyndar drew a blaster.

"I see."

"You talk too much."

"I hear that a lot." Carl knew he was safe. Maybe this guy could stun him, but even then, it was more than likely that the guard would be in for hell if he did.

"You were once a great enemy of my people."

Oh, so this was all just a chat at blasterpoint. Carl had really gotten over those by now. "Sure. You guys make me look good out there. Weeping. Sobbing. Drooling. My COs barely put up with me, but you guys are building me a legacy."

"There is a riot outside. They think you're getting off easy."

"Their opinions and mine vary on a wide range of topics."

The guard snickered. "They are merely impatient. Your deaths will bring glory to Emperor Grudrak."

"I still don't like that plural."

The guard ignored him. "That, we cannot abide."

"Wait. What?"

Something had gone wrong. Carl felt it in his bones. He had one more day of verbal beatings from the bereaved relatives of his Typhoon-era victims before they were scheduled to spend half a day half drowning him. He already had a Carl Who Was Convinced He Could Breathe Water ready to go.

But this guard who'd smuggled a blaster into a no-blasters-near-the-prisoner zone wasn't on board Emperor Grudrak's ship.

"Be at peace, friend. Your quick, quiet, private death will be a great loss for Emperor Grudrak. I won't survive this, either. My life and yours... for the good of the empire." He shouted the last without so much as raising his voice.

"Hold on a sec! We can—"

Carl lunged. Arm outstretched to its limit, he couldn't reach the blaster before it fired.

———

Shuttle 1 sank beneath the surface of the wastewater treatment center. Jessie did *not* envy the maintenance team who had to clean out the crevices and ramp mechanicals.

The pair marched through the facility, culling workers along the way. Jessie pitched hers into the murky depths to get caught in the filters they were responsible for maintaining. Hadrian vanished one in a show of both magical brute force and startling subtlety.

There one second. Gone the next, he'd told her. Hadrian being Mordecai The Brown was getting both easier to see and harder to ignore.

When they reached ground level, they found themselves in the midst of a celebration.

The city streets of This Is Here bustled Mardi Gras energy, minus the whimsy. Eyndar music reminiscent of yodeling brought back dusty old memories of Carson Colony campfire sing-alongs. Darkness reigned in the sky far overhead, but technological lighting beat it back with iron lamp posts and spiderwebs of colored bistro lights spanning the gaps between concrete buildings.

But the colors were all blues and yellows and browns. The festival was the kind of place that ancient Soviet gulags would have found too depressing.

"Move. Move. Move," a civil defense soldier ordered, sweeping an arm repeatedly to herd the crowd forward. The flow of eyndar revelers carried them off in a direction other than toward the prison.

Communicating via body language and eye contact, the pair accepted the forced shift in their planned route.

When the opportunity arose, Jessie got them back on track, diverting course through a bistro that would have been a Slurp'n'Burp in border space but went by its eyndar name here that translated to Bowl Chow.

On the streets on the other side of the restaurant, the pair managed to veer back toward the military prison.

Upon encountering a raucous crowd outside, protesting Dad's fairly benign treatment as unjust to them somehow, Hadrian bullied their way through and into the place like they were arriving to file a complaint.

No justice without blood, the crowd was chanting outside.

Jessie suspected that Hadrian's justice would involve more of a light ash and a lingering scent.

"State your business," a prison bureaucrat at the front desk instructed brusquely.

Hadrian's eyndar was impeccable, even if his accent leaned Back Bay Bostonian. "We're here to see the human."

"There are no visitors allowed. Only guards and medical staff are permitted access. Begone."

Hadrian pulled down his mask such that his eyes met those of the astonished administrator. "Make an exception."

Canine eyes glazed over. Pupils shrank all the way shut. "Yes. I will. Summon. An escort."

Two uniformed guards arrived, one concealing a small

blaster under his uniform. An odd detail, but since Jessie no longer feared blaster fire, she tucked it away as irrelevant.

Down they delved into the outdated prison that somehow felt all the more secure for its lack of data vulnerability.

Halfway down, a commotion rose.

Panicked eyndar shouts of confusion revealed nothing but a security breach in progress.

"Shall we?" Mort asked in plain English.

"Huh?" a guard inquired as the pair herded Mort and Jessie out of the way as booted feet raced up from below.

Jessie gave a nod.

The jig was up.

Hadrian waved a hand and the two guards vanished in twin flashes of fire.

Pulling off the mask and tucking it under one arm, he led the way onward.

"Do you know where you're going?" Jessie demanded, now lugging her mask as spare baggage as well. She'd learned this layout from every entry point and found it hard to believe the wizard had bothered memorizing the whole thing.

Rather than answer in words, Hadrian stepped aside and allowed her to take point.

"Intruder!"

"Sound the alarm!"

"Lock down the building!"

"So much for getting to him first," Jessie griped, breaking into a run that slowed only to punch and kick steel-barred doors that blocked their path.

Hadrian fell behind as he slowed to make quick work of the guards as they responded to the alarm.

Jessie raced all the way to the prison cell where Dad was being kept.

She saw the body. Her fist blasted through the lock,

slamming the barred door open. She skidded to Dad's side on her knees.

"No... NO!!!" Jessie wailed over the still, lifeless form of Carl Ramsey on the floor of his cell.

⸺

Eric waited in the hangar.

He didn't play Go Fish.

Either Jessie and Hadrian were coming back with Dad alive this time or, more likely, things were going to turn out the same as before.

He hadn't changed enough. He hadn't *done* enough. Sitting here awaiting the return of Shuttle 1 was his penance.

But this wasn't over yet. Whether some uncontrollable variable of fate shook the dice a little differently and Dad came out OK despite Eric's failure or whether the events played out just as he remembered, Eric still had more to learn.

Suddenly, over at the Logistics poker game, heads popped up. Datapads whipped out. The players scattered in a flurry of overlapping chatter that even Eric's practiced ear couldn't decipher.

Knowing he had time enough, Eric took a brisk walk over to the lift and waited.

The hangar floor irised open. Grosstet's shuttle breached the glowing blue surface like a dolphin, beaching itself just meters from Eric with its back end toward the lift.

Lift doors parted. Britney and Harmony had a hover stretcher. Jessie flopped Dad onto it and followed the pair back into the lift.

This time, Eric didn't follow.

The doors shut as Jessie was trying to explain how she'd

found Dad unresponsive on the floor of an eyndar prison mere minutes ago.

Eric wanted answers his sister was in no position to give.

"What happened?" he demanded of the one who remained behind.

"Got there too late," Hadrian grumbled, eyes like storm clouds, not even looking in Eric's direction. "Damned eyndar did him in early."

Before he could wander off into the noble grief of the Hero Who Tried and Failed, Eric stepped directly into Hadrian's path. "No. Details. From the minute you left, as quick as you can recount it."

Hadrian cast a shrewd glare Eric's way. "You aren't planning on traveling back and undoing this, are you?"

"Let's assume for the sake of argument that I'm not. I just need to know."

The youthful elder wizard didn't appear convinced, but explaining things was in his bones to the marrow. "Jess missed the entry. Right in the damned ocean. Spaceship knew how to doggy paddle, but it cost us time. Got through the toilet tank just fine, but topside, they'd turned your dad's execution into an all-night street festival, complete with live entertainment and crowd-control goons. We got controlled a little before ducking through a Slurp'n'Burp—"

"They still have those?"

"I'll pick you up a garlic butter bowl next time I'm there."

Eric was tempted to hold him to that, but the request sounded almost too flippant to pose, even. "Then what?"

"Scrambled a brain or two inside the prison. Got escorted down to see Carl. There was a commotion, and the alarm went up before we'd even done anything. Murdered our way down to his cell and found him like we brought him back."

It was very Mordecai The Brown of Hadrian to use "murder" as a verb of motion. "Thanks."

"Knowing doesn't make it any easier. Does it?"

Eric shook his head.

"And you're not going to go off on some half-cocked scheme to reverse the natural flow of time, potentially wiping us all out, to see if you can save him..."

Eric couldn't help a grin. Hadrian's furious scowl crackled with lightning. "Too late. Thanks for your—"

A fork fell with a clatter that rang through the dining lounge.

IT ALL STARTS HERE

Clearly, Eric hadn't done enough. He'd sniffed around, poked his nose in places, and lurked around corners listening to the planning and final preparations for Dad's rescue, and in the end, nothing he'd done had really made a difference.

Hadrian's words, from mere moments ago, wouldn't be spoken until sometime late tomorrow. But Eric premembered them.

A missed landing coming out of astral. A festival delaying the approach to the prison. If he could smooth those out, maybe then he'd start seeing some results. Oh, and getting Jessie off her ass and into that shuttle earlier wouldn't hurt, either.

But first, Eric finished his pancakes.

There was something about starting off this loop yet again that made his mistreatment of the meal seem almost an original sin. Like, maybe if he took his time, ate what he'd ordered, and proceeded on a full stomach, maybe he'd find better results.

He couldn't rush this, not any of it. Time would keep

looping until he got it right, and in aiming for a bullseye, he wasn't even hitting the dartboard. Or pitching a bowling ball so hard down a lane in hopes of a strike that it slammed into the gutter and lobbed into an adjacent lane, getting you and your brother and sister and your laaku cousins kicked out of the alley.

No. Eric was going to tinker. Not just tinker... *intervene.* Stuff was going to change this time around.

But first, a washroom. That had been quite a large mug of coffee.

———

Two wizards intertwined, joined by the most primal of biological acts and wet with comingled sweat. On and off—mostly on—for the past hour, they'd enjoyed the privacy of one another's company undisturbed.

Sparta Dahl's job here, if she wished to prolong the encounter, was to occupy the massive intellect of the man pinned beneath her hips and thighs. Raw lust could devour them both like a feast for the starving. And a puzzle or conundrum would be solved faster than she could compose one.

But no mind, no matter how mighty, could overcome the sopping dead weight of small talk. Not even Hadrian The Brown.

Between various intermissions, they'd discussed travel holovids, the personal lives of their fellow passengers aboard the *Arete*, and gift ideas for the upcoming birthdays of various relations. Presently, she was fencing with him over the benefits of a tesud diet.

"If you have the... nuts in it... you don't get that... empty feeling of being... hungry after a meal..."

Hadrian's oratory skills were presently failing him. "Fair enough. Just... let's see... about how often we eat salad."

"I could definitely—" Sparta's whole body stiffened, and her mind clung to the insides of her skull as a torrent of visions washed past her.

"If you need me to move my fingers, I can certainly—"

Sparta's mouth opened, but she lacked breath to give voice to words. Taking the cue entirely amiss, Hadrian finished, continuing for her benefit alone.

When the visions passed, they lingered. Leaning back down, she clung to her lover, digging nails into his shoulders in a desperate attempt to hang on. A hand came up and cupped her cheek, brushing aside the thin chain running from her right nostril to her earlobe.

A wave of calm settled over her as the hallucinations faded. All she saw was Hadrian, concerned yet unwilling to stop his efforts without her direction.

Her mind needed a reset. The solution was already halfway implemented.

Once her own climax came and passed, she slumped down on the pillow, regaining her breath and radiating heat in waves.

"You all right?"

"*Eenok tra'raal*," Sparta replied.

Hadrian snickered. "My business is making sure that was blissful release and not a metaphysical seizure you just had there. And when did you start learning eyndar?"

"Eyndar?"

"Yeah. You just told me to 'state my business,' in possibly the worst eyndar accent I've ever heard."

Leaning over, she poked a finger into Hadrian's bare chest. "*N'taang omo grinmaw*. What does that mean?"

"'We're here to see the human.' Did you just have a vision? The future?"

A headache clamped on as if a set of those giant haathee doors slammed with Sparta's head between them. "I don't know how to describe it. An echo?"

"From the past or the future?"

Her thoughts refused to clear. "I don't know. Both? I don't know how; it *feels* like a past but looks like the future. Can you just... make it go away for a while?"

"I thought you hated that."

"*Make an exception.*" It wasn't eyndar this time. She'd parroted an echo of the Golden Voice, the universal magical language that spoke directly to the mind, bypassing concepts of nouns and verbs and grammar and conveying meaning in defiance of species, culture, and biological vocalization.

As a gentle willpower overwhelmed her, the pain eased. The echoes faded. The tension seeped from every muscle in her body.

Sparta shifted and sighed and curled up beside her lover, coaxing an arm around her and interrupting the gradual drying process of two sweaty bodies. "Much better. Just hold me, mind and body."

"How long do you need?"

In her physical relief, her humor had returned. "I should be asking *you* that."

━━━

Eric knocked.

Trebla's door slid open.

"Hey, Eric. Come on in," Jasmine told him. She was in her underwear, taming her hair into a ponytail that looked more like a foundation brush, given how short she kept it.

"You know, you could put clothes on first," Trebla griped.

"Or let me. He knows how to wait." Across the room, Eric's laaku cousin was hopping into his engineering coveralls.

Jasmine caught her own mechanic's attire when Trebla lobbed it her way.

"I didn't mean to interrupt."

"You didn't," Jasmine assured him. "That's the beauty of a quickie. It's quick. I've got stuff to do. Treb's got his own shit to deal with. It's like a battery recharge." She slipped her feet into pantlegs, then zipped the whole thing up without Eric even noticing how her arms ended up in the sleeves. In an instant, she was all but dressed and finished off by stepping into a pair of workboots that self-cinched.

"Lunch?" Trebla called after her.

Jasmine sized up her roommate as she retrieved gloves and goggles from a table beside the door. "I'll think about it." With a grin and a wink, she departed.

"What?" Trebla snapped. "Can't a guy have a quiet mid-morning tryst in peace?"

"I'd have waited if I'd known," Eric countered.

"Well... whatever. You're here now. Make it quick. I've got shit I promised Jessie and I'm behind schedule."

"Tell her it can't be done," Eric ordered firmly.

"Um. It can. And it will. And since when do you even care?"

"Jessie's going to be late. She won't be in time to rescue Dad. You need to let her know that these new glovey-doodads aren't something she should wait for."

Trebla put an arm around Eric's waist and guided him toward the door. "I get it. I'm worried about Uncle Carl, too. But everything's going to be—"

"I've created a time loop where every time we fail to save Dad I go back to like half an hour ago and this time I'm trying to get a head start on saving him for good."

"Eric, are you feeling all right?"

"If I were to ask you for a password, you'd say 'Eric, you're an idiot,' without actually meaning for it to be a password."

"OK. Fine. But, I mean, you *are* being one."

"And you and Jasmine just tried something called a lemon juicer."

"WHAT? Are you fucking spying on us?"

"No!" Eric protested, offended by the implication. "I just remember from the day after yestertomorrow that she voice-commed you to set up what I just came in at the end of."

"Eric... I'm going to say this slowly so you don't mishear it. Go. See. Charlotte. Whatever it is she does for you, have her do it. She's the only one qualified to deal with"—Trebla waved three hands in Eric's general direction—"*this*, right now."

A determined frown settled onto Eric's features. "Fine."

"Good."

"On *one* condition."

Trebla groaned, which was more than mildly insulting. One condition wasn't a whole lot to ask, and he was otherwise being given an ultimatum, which wasn't exactly the height of not-being-rude in the first place. "Fine. What condition?"

"I want a password. A *real* password. Something that you'll only give me this once, that you'll know came from you, and can convince you next time there's a loop that I'm telling the truth."

The *Arete's* chief engineer paused, narrowing one eye and giving the matter genuine thought, if Eric was any judge. "All right. Here goes. Uncle Carl swore me to secrecy, so either he dies or I never told you anything, got it?"

"That's the password?"

"No. I just need your word, first."

"Fine. You have it."

"Kay. Here goes. You didn't not get a cake on your eleventh

birthday because Uncle Carl forgot. He broke Dad's guitar messing with the tuning as a prank and used the money for your cake to pay for a quick-repair shop to patch it up before the band's gig that night. I caught him in the act, but he swore me to secrecy."

"But I *did* have a cake for my eleventh birthday." Eric didn't have a clear recollection of that specific birthday, but all through his childhood, there'd always been cakes.

"You did. Three days later at our next stop."

Something wasn't adding up. "How come you didn't tell?" Swearing things was only semi-binding for wizards. To everyone else, a promise was a transient noise on the wind.

"I'm going to decline to answer that, time-travel boy. If you hit me with that one, I might—just *might*—believe you got that info from another timeline."

That evening, Charlotte was lying in wait when Eric got home.

"Oh. Hi. Didn't expect to find you here. Thought you had therapy sessions."

"Aubrey canceled," Charlotte stated. She was still wearing her therapist uniform. It wasn't his favorite look of hers, but it was better than her bridge uniform. In the Village of Eternity, she seemed more herself in loose pants and a trim, sleeveless top. Her best real-world look had stuck in his mind the day he'd met her, campus casual in a sweatshirt and a skirt with clogs.

"Are you mad at me?" Eric asked. Something felt off about the air in the room.

"I haven't decided. I'd like to hear your side of why, as the commanding officer for much of this crew, I'm fielding complaints about you from across the ship."

Well, it *had* been a busy day. And from a certain

perspective, Eric could see how maybe some of the people he spoke to might have felt bothered. That was one of the pitfalls of this *Wissen geht vor* approach to the current loop. He was stepping on toes that wouldn't be sore next time around.

If what he learned was important enough, he'd weather this storm.

Charlotte wasn't liable to remember this conversation anyway. And if she did, it was because this loop somehow managed to save Dad. He could live with that. Eric had a lot of practice with apologies.

"You want the truth?"

Charlotte's eyebrows rose. "I would be *delighted* with the truth."

"I doubt it," Eric replied ruefully. "You might want to sit down."

"I'll stand."

Oh. This was going to be one of *those* conversations. The two of them had a dynamic. Emergent. Never stated out loud. But in the Village of Eternity, Eric was a god. Suns rose and set at his whim. He drafted laws of physics the way a junior city councilman drafted new ordinances. But out in the real world, Charlotte was the responsible one, the one who took on decisions that might have consequences, especially dire ones.

Eric was stronger than her here, too, of course, but only magically. He lacked her confidence, her surety, her focus, and her sense of purpose. Eric drifted through life, and if Charlotte steered the boat, he didn't grab for the rudder.

Today, it seemed, Charlotte had a firm hand on the tiller.

"OK. To start with, you've known I'm a chronomancer for a while now."

"Eric..."

"I'm just saying, you didn't sign on with a guy who you knew for a fact hadn't tinkered with time travel. Just like I knew you could do that scary thing with your eyebrows that you're doing right now before agreeing to share a bed with you."

"Eeeeeriiiiiic..."

"So, thinking that there was a good chance that an entire Eyndar Empire wanted Dad dead and two well-meaning but less-than-numerous people were planning to go by themselves to save him, I set up a contingency where I assured the universe that Carl Ramsey couldn't possibly die in the Eyndar Empire and that any timeline where that happened was fake."

"ERIC!" Charlotte bellowed. "How could you?!"

"I mean... until Dad died the first time, and everything went back to this morning, I wasn't sure that I had. But the 'how' is simple. We already covered that part. I'm a chronomancer."

"Thought so," Hadrian grumbled as he emerged from the washroom. "Your four-handed cousin came to me in a state, yammering about time loops. Worried you'd gone bonkers. More worried you hadn't."

"You don't understand the forces you're playing with," Charlotte explained. "This is for your own good."

Magic ceased. For a split second, Eric guessed that it was somehow her doing.

But, no.

"You can come along quietly or loudly, but you're headed for the brig," Hadrian informed him.

"The brig?"

Eric had been in the brig before, but that was in the old days—months ago! The old Hadrian had rigged up a crazy series of interlocking runes, but Eric knew that the new Hadrian had been fiddling with them as a side project for his own boredom.

"You won't put up a magical fight. Not with her help. Certainly not without it. And, odd as it may feel to say it, I'm bigger than you, stronger than you, and not above dragging your wimpy ass down there by the collar of your shirt."

Eric flinched when Hadrian marched toward him. "You don't need to—"

"Don't you *dare* try launching me into the future. I don't care if you think this is a time loop and that there are no consequences, but imagine that the loop resets but I've been sent beyond it. Do I vanish retroactively from the timeline? Would there be two of me on the other side, once the loop resolves?"

At first, Eric didn't know the reason for Hadrian's ire. Then, it occurred to him that the outflung hand meant to physically ward him off might have been interpreted as a prelude to a contact-based magical attack.

"I'll... I don't know. I won't try anything."

Hadrian harrumphed. "Good."

The trio marched down to the brig together. Charlotte maintained an icy silence, failing to intervene on his behalf the whole way down.

That was how Eric knew she was mad at him. Really mad. Not miffed. Charlotte had a wide range of miff that spanned from breakfast pranks gone awry to embarrassing public behavior.

When he stepped through the door and into the specialized wizard-proof cell, he couldn't help but notice that *all* the runes looked new and unfamiliar. He hadn't checked since... well, he couldn't recall checking at all down here since Hadrian came back with a different wizard in him.

Red, angry, and flaring to life as soon as he was caged within, Eric found that even Hadrian's suppression of his magic had been kind by comparison.

When she saw his grimace of pain, Charlotte finally intervened. "The cell seems to be hurting him."

"Probably," Hadrian agreed. "But nothing that'll cause permanent harm. Maybe teach him a lesson. We'll see about getting out of this loop. If not, maybe I can find some way to convey information or hold onto memories of these events like he no doubt is."

"Could you ensorcell him to impart memories back to you?"

Hadrian rubbed his chin. "Morphean technique. I know *nothing* about those. But I can give it a try."

Eric backed away from the cell door. "You're not magicking me up with your memories."

"I'm not asking."

Eric panicked.

This could ruin everything. The last thing he needed— could afford, even—was an adversary dogging his every loop.

Racing the two paces to the back of the cell, Eric hit his head and knocked himself out cold.

A fork fell with a clatter that rang through the dining lounge.

IT ALL STARTS HERE

Eric breathed a sigh of relief. Partially that his desperate plan seemed to have worked. Partially because he didn't wake up with a splitting headache and a spell boring its way into his psyche.

Dad must have died. Whether Eric's self-inflicted injury had been fatal or not, Eric didn't need to know.

His highly invasive questioning had taught him some new details. One, time was a bit harder to steer than he'd imagined. Two, he'd started the loop later than might otherwise have been helpful. Three, Hadrian The Brown was a raging asshole.

Uncle Enzio had been a cranky, irascible middle-aged

grouch, a codger ahead of his years. Plunked into a youthful body and cut free from the tethers of needing Mom to not want him evicted from the *Mobius*, he was showing truer colors (and less tolerance for Eric) than he'd ever shown before.

Or maybe futzing around with time really just *was* that bad and Eric needed to accept that.

What Eric *didn't* need to accept was that Jessie's plan was the only option.

Given his lack of success in altering the course of hers, Eric had his own plan.

Which was Jessie's with a different crew and quicker timeline.

Knowing that he had "lemon juicer" to wait out, and suspecting that Trebla's mood would be better afterward rather than before, Eric enjoyed a leisurely pancake meal and cleaned up after his own dishes.

Then, he headed over and knocked on Trebla's door.

No answer.

He tried again with no better luck. If anything, the prior loops had shown him that Trebla and Jasmine were both more than willing to answer the door, ready or not, knowing it was him or not.

They weren't home.

Crap. He'd waited too long. Not that Jasmine's absence was a problem. Eric had been counting on that. If there was one thing a significant other was good for, it was the application of kibosh to a bold and daring plan.

Belatedly, Eric tried to reverse engineer a letter for this plan and decided to start from scratch.

This was now Eric's Rescue: Plan A.

Luckily, the Plan B alteration only required Eric to venture to Trebla's test lab. He ran into Jomek along the way but studiously chose to limit himself to an exchange of pleasantries.

Eric knocked but let himself in through the lab's open door. "Am I interrupting anything?"

"Kinda," Trebla replied without looking up from his work. "This anything that can wait?"

"Yes, in a way. But no, in a more important way."

"Make that make sense and I'll give you five minutes," Trebla countered.

This was it. "I'm a time-traveling version of Eric that managed to come back two days in time to recruit you for a mission to save Dad because Jessie's plan is going to fail."

Trebla blinked as he focused on Eric instead of his embiggenating view double-telescope thing. "Wow. You been hanging out with Figgy? What's he pack the hookah with?"

"Dad swore you to secrecy about my eleventh birthday cake. He broke your dad's guitar and needed the money to fix it before Uncle Roddy noticed."

"How'd you find that out? I never told anyone!"

"You did. Previous loop. I *think* it was just last loop, but really, these things are getting a little muddy in my head."

"Whoa."

"Whoa, indeed. You told me that you'd believe me if I told you that, and... it's looking like maybe you do?"

Trebla flicked switches. Indicator lights on his workbench blinked off. "OK. I'll admit that does *sound* like something I might have used as a secret code. But why should I believe you that it's time travel and not a mind-reading trick or I got high and told Jessie or something and it got back to you. Or if Uncle Carl just flat-out fessed up at some point."

"Never confess," Eric quoted. Trebla joined him in reciting the second half of Dad's mantra. "Make them prove it to a jury or it didn't happen."

Trebla relented. "Yeah. I know. Doesn't sound like Uncle

Carl. But still, it sounds less crazy than you getting real, like, Hollyworld-grade time traveling working."

"You promised you'd believe me," Eric protested.

"Well, maybe I lied. Newsfeed: sometimes it's easier lying to people than seeing their shit through to the end. Love ya, Eric, but you're right at the top of that list."

"Oh."

"Oh, don't be like that! You come in here, singing a weird tune about time travel loops and shit and just expect me to believe the most outrageous of a million possible explanations?"

"But... it's about trusting me. You don't trust me. Do you?"

"I would loan you money but not go with you on time travel adventures. I don't know where the line is exactly that I wouldn't cross, but it's between those somewhere. Oh. And just what *were* you thinking I'd help you with?"

Piloting me to the eyndar homeworld, just like Jessie was going to do for Hadrian. The words were on the tip of Eric's tongue, but he realized that saying them was going to be the effective end of this loop.

"Doesn't matter. You're right. I'll just sit back and wait it out."

"Good man. Now, back to some *real* work."

Eric slunk out of Trebla's lab with an echo in his mind.

Sometimes it's easier lying to people than seeing their shit through to the end.

———

"AH, ERIC, MY FRIEND. ENTER. JOIN ME FOR A SOAK."

There was frivolity, then there was humoring a friend when about to ask a favor, then there was climbing into a hot tub with a ten-foot-tall elephant because he had the best one on the *Arete*.

"Ahhh," Eric sighed. The relaxing warmth seeped in through his pores. If he got tuckered out or frustrated, taking a break here after a bad loop might rejuvenate his sense of purpose.

"TO WHAT DO I OWE THE VAST PLEASURE OF YOUR COMPANY?"

Eric considered how to phrase his answer. Unlike so many of the crew, Grosstet paid attention to words. "Commiseration."

"INDEED? WHAT MISERIES MIGHT WE SHARE WITH ONE ANOTHER?" Grosstet used his trunk to blow bigger bubbles than the tub's jets already provided. Eric wasn't going to comment on the fact that the bubbles were all coming up from around his nethers.

"Well, for starters, that neither of us made the A team for rescuing my father."

"I DID OFFER MY SERVICES AS A PILOT. OUR CAPTAIN CHOSE THE YOUNG WIZARD AS THE ASSAULT FORCE AND HERSELF AS THE DELIVERYPERSON."

"They're going to fail, you know."

"ARE THEY, NOW? HAVE YOU BEEN SPEAKING WITH THE NEWCOMER, WIZARD SPARTA?"

"No. I've seen the future because I've been there."

"REALLY? I THOUGHT YOU AND YOUR SISTER HAD BOTH MADE IT CLEAR THAT YOU HAD SKIPPED SOME OF THE PAST, NOT COME FROM THE FUTURE."

"That was then, this is now," Eric argued. "When I said that, it was true. Circumstances have changed. Now, I'm asking for your help, as a friend, as an adventurer, as a hero, to help me save my father from otherwise certain doom."

Grosstet placed one flat palm on his bare chest, then folded the other atop it, right above his heart. "I AM HONORED AND HUMBLED. HOW MUST WE PROCEED? YOU HAVE SEEN THE FAILINGS OF THE OTHER PLAN, CORRECT?"

"They're too late. The eyndar kill my father before Jessie and Hadrian get there, and try as I might, I can't get them to hurry the heck up. If we leave soon—now, if possible—and head straight for the prison where they're keeping him, we ought to be able to get there in plenty of time. I don't think Jessie and Hadrian are crazy late. Harmony said something about him being dead hours. We'll get there the day before he's going to die. You in?"

"I WAS 'IN' WHEN YOU ASKED FOR A HERO."

———

Getting Shuttle 1 off the *Arete* was a *ton* easier than Eric had imagined. If he ever decided to skedaddle and start life over on the lam as a fugitive from being a fugitive, Grosstet was the guy to have along. Of course, the fact that the more colloquial name for Shuttle 1 was "Grosstet's Shuttle" didn't hurt either. Built entirely from H-tech, beyond all but the basic understanding of the scruffy old laaku mechanic they'd chased out of it, and with access codes only available to a fluent speaker of a language that required a trunk to enunciate properly, he was the ideal pilot for it.

An adapter chair lay disconnected in the back.

Eric sat on the arm of the copilot's seat.

Grosstet handled the controls like an old pro. Which, Eric realized, he technically was.

Astral space whirled all around them, nearly purple, Eric had shot them so far down into it.

Not a light or hum survived the transit.

"So, while we wait, let's review the plan. You remember what my father looks like, right?"

"I RECALL HIS FACE WELL. HOWEVER, I ALSO SURMISE THAT, GIVEN THE STATE OF THE EYNDAR EMPIRE AT PRESENT, HE WILL BE POSSIBLY THE ONLY HUMAN BESIDES YOURSELF WE ARE LIABLE TO ENCOUNTER."

"That, too. OK. So, you've got all the maps that Jessie and Lisa and Mindy and Daphne have been piecing together. We're going to use those to find the right spot to land."

"THEY HAVE DISCUSSED THE COORDINATES AT LENGTH."

"And Jessie and Hadrian were going to miss anyway," Eric added. "We're going to have to do better than them."

Grosstet's trunk flicked. "I AM A SUPERIOR PILOT TO JESSICA. I HAVE PILOTED VESSELS LIKE THIS SINCE BEFORE THE BIRTH OF YOUR FATHER. I... I BELIEVE. YOUR FATHER, IS HE LESS THAN NINETY-THREE YEARS OLD?"

"Comfortably."

"THEN MY STATEMENT STANDS! WE SHALL PREVAIL WHERE THE OTHERS WOULD HAVE FAILED."

"*Will* failed," Eric corrected.

"I DO NOT THINK YOU APPLY YOUR ALTERNATIVE TO PROPER GRAMMAR WITH ANY CONSISTENCY WHATSOEVER. WE SHALL AVERT THE FAILED TIMELINE."

A whoosh of air suggested that Shuttle 1 was getting over its magical hiccup.

"Averting, we shall go!" It turned into a little song after a repetition and the addition of a few hi-hos, with Grosstet joining in as he picked up on the simplistic lyrics and melody.

After all, why loop time into a pretzel if you couldn't have some fun with the fact that failure only gained you another try?

Eric had been failing all his life. Youth sports, family game nights, colonial schools, crafts projects, his sleight of hand talent show act where the fine print forbade magic, college, being ship's wizard of the *Arete*. Eric was an expert at failing.

This venture only needed one success.

The sing-along died out as the last of the shuttle's systems returned to normal functioning.

"OUR ESTIMATED TRAVEL TIME IS NEARLY AN HOUR."

"Any suggestions for how you'd like to spend it?"

"YOUR FATHER. YOU HAVE SPOKEN OF HIM OCCASIONALLY, AND I HAVE MET HIM AND CONVERSED AT LENGTH ON THOSE OCCASIONS. YET I STILL FEEL AS IF I DO NOT KNOW HIM."

"I could tell you a story or two."

"THAT WOULD BE A DELIGHT."

⸺

As it turned out, Eric could be long-winded. Two stories got them to the eyndar homeworld. One involved Dad remaining calm as the venue he was playing caught fire. On the fly, he got the band to switch to a song called *Burning Down the House* before authorities cleared everyone out. The other story was of the time Mom was sick, so Eric and Ozzy went with him to a local clinic to pick up supplies for the *Mobius's* depleted med kit. The trip involved a stop-off and an exchange of data crystals for hardcoin with some scary-looking guys in suits; but the clinic wasn't the free sort, and Mom had a fever, so Dad maybe didn't color inside the lines that one time.

"HERD BEFORE GOVERNOR. HERDS AND GOVERNORS PREFER THAT EVERYONE AGREES ON RIGHT AND WRONG, BUT WHEN THEY CONFLICT, I AGREE WITH YOUR FATHER. WE HAVE ARRIVED WHERE THE PLANET WOULD BE IF THIS WERE REALSPACE. WHAT PRECAUTIONS SHALL WE TAKE TO OUTWIT OUR FOES AND BEST OUR TEMPORALLY ASYNCHRONOUS COMPETITION?"

No one was competing at anything since there was only one Shuttle 1 with super haathee gadgets, but Eric understood the jab at Jessie and Hadrian for their doomed attempts.

"Well, Hadrian said they landed in the ocean, and they were aiming for a water-cleaning factory at the shoreline. I say we aim right for the plaza where they're having their big event, then when we miss, we'll be closer."

"WE WILL NOT MISS."

"It's not you. It's me. Magic's only so precise. We're skydiving onto a merry-go-round at night in a blizzard and the horses buck."

"YOU HAVE USED TOO DENSE A METAPHOR. REST ASSURED, HOWEVER, THAT WE WILL NOT MISS."

"Just aim us at the central plaza where all the yelling at Dad is taking place. I don't know what time it'll be there, but—"

"APPROXIMATELY TWO HOURS PAST NOON."

"Even better. Why sneak Dad out of a deep, dark prison when we can grab him off the stage when everyone can see that he's not the bad guy and that nice people care about him and are willing to risk their lives—or at least a resetting of their timelines—to save him. Not that we'll explain about the time loop. That can be our secret. But the rest, yeah. Let's land."

"WE SHALL SWOOP LIKE A DUCK HUNTING ITS PREY. I SHALL SWING AROUND WITH THE RAMP OPEN. YOU BREAK ANY SHACKLES WITH MAGIC. WE SHALL BE GONE BEFORE THE EYNDAR KNOW HOW TO REACT."

"Let's do this! Tell me when you've got us in position. I'll bring us back to realspace."

Thick fingers and a deft trunk worked technology as foreign to Eric as magic must have been to the haathee. In no time at all, Grosstet reported back.

"I HAVE MATCHED US TO THE PLANET'S ROTATION. RELATIVE TO THE GROUND, WE WOULD APPEAR STATIONARY."

Eric had an inkling of how planets rolled through space in multiple dimensions. "That sounds hard."

"FOR SOME, IT WOULD BE."

"Let me know when you want us to drop back."

"AS I SAID, WE ARE, FROM THE PLANET'S PERSPECTIVE, FIXED IN PLACE ABOVE OUR DESTINATION. RE-ENTER STANDARD REALITY AT YOUR CONVENIENCE."

Here goes nothing.

Whoooosh!

———

The bellowing of a trumpet sounded the alarm as Grosstet panicked at the controls.

Eric, preoccupied with covering his ears and adjusting to the pressure change in the cabin. A split second later, he realized that there was sky outside the front window.

And they were falling.

Eric wasn't strapped in. He chose not to be in freefall. Grabbing hold of the back of the copilot's chair in one hand and Grosstet's shoulder in the other, he held on for the brief, tech-free journey from sky to ground.

Shuttle 1 struck like an asteroid. A cloud of dust obscured all vision around them.

"ARE YOU INJURED?"

"No. I don't think so. Good shuttle."

"IT MAY BE GOOD AGAIN, BUT PRESENTLY IT IS A HOLLOW BOX AND NOTHING MORE. WE MUST MAKE HASTE AND TRUST THAT THE SHUTTLE WILL RECOVER IN TIME FOR OUR RETURN. WE HAVE YOUR FATHER TO SAVE."

"Right. The mission."

Eric forced the ramp open. Grosstet picked up his ginormous handgun, which presumably would work again soon. In the meantime, it would be up to Eric to protect them both and see to Dad's safe recovery.

A summoned wind cleared the air around the shuttle's crash site.

They'd hit smack dab in the middle of the plaza they were aiming for. True to his word, Grosstet hadn't missed.

The plaza had become a disaster zone. Bodies lay bloody and still near the impact crater. Spectators continued to flee the scene. A horizontal rain of blaster fire assailed them, shots pinwheeling away as they neared Eric and his protectee.

"DAD!" Eric shouted when he spotted the lone human, chained atop a raised platform accessible by a long series of stairs, placing him over the crowd. Beneath, a slowly spinning paddle swept rotten fruit and a startling number of shoes into a waste reclaim chute.

"ERIC?" Dad called back, hoarse but audible. "What are you doing here?"

Knowing there was never a right time to be serious and businesslike when it came to Dad, Eric answered, "Sightseeing. Heard there was a festival. Wanted to see about the fuss."

The joke may have drawn a smile from Dad, but the time for levity was fast ending.

Eric felt them.

Wizards.

A lot of wizards.

Weaklings, individually, but there were a lot of them. They poured from the nearby structure that Jessie's briefings had claimed was the eyndar equivalent of a Convocation. Eric could have squelched a dozen of them without effort. A score might have worked up a mental sweat to overcome. But Eric was running out of archaic units to describe the number now converging on them.

A bushel?

A gaggle?

Lots-n-lots-n-lots? That one held some promise in adequately summarizing the opposition he felt. Gulliver the wizard had found his Lilliputians, and they had their thread-like ropes out.

"Get me loose!" Dad ordered, tugging against the chains at his wrists and ankles as if to demonstrate why he wasn't already running to get down from the platform and make his way to Shuttle 1.

Eric clenched a fist. He wanted to break steel links, snap cuffs, turn Dad momentarily insubstantial. Nothing. Nothing worked.

"MY WEAPON SEEMS TO HAVE RECOVERED. I WILL FREE CARL; YOU CATCH HIM BEFORE HE LANDS."

Grosstet brought up his horrific weapon and aimed at the catwalk that supported the platform. It was, to be fair to the impromptu Plan Q or so, the fastest way to get Dad to the ground. The beam of shimmering anti-stuff ripped through the structure like a baseball through a birthday cake.

However, unable to work the simplest of magics for the veritable oodle of eyndar wizards reporting to the crash site, Eric could only watch in helpless shock as Dad plummeted three stories to the plaza stonework, unable even to jump clear or shield himself to mitigate the impact.

He witnessed the splat.

Blaster fire poured in. Grosstet used his bulk and the belt-mounted starship shield to protect them both.

"ERIC, I THOUGHT YOU WOULD MAGIC HIM."

"I... I can't."

Eric stared. Dad groaned.

He was alive!

Racing out of cover, Eric didn't stand a chance. Before he could make it halfway to his father—

A fork fell with a clatter that rang through the dining lounge.

IT ALL STARTS HERE

The rescue attempt on his own had been a disaster. And it was a disaster in five more loops afterward, all in a similar vein.

The next loop, Eric had simply tried to work around the surprise appearance in the plaza (and improve the lyrics of his song), but the eyndar had still overwhelmed them.

An attempt to enter realspace more slowly must have thrown Grosstet's calculated orbit off kilter, because they dropped out of astral in a magma chamber far below the planet's surface and hadn't lasted much beyond their arrival.

After that, Eric had tried arriving later, but an assault on the prison just drew a blockade from the eyndar corps of wizards, and they died again.

Smaller variation yielded depressingly repetitive results.

Dead. Dead. And more dead.

Sometimes Dad died and it just reset the loop. Other times, Eric was killed and couldn't tell the difference. Oddly—or maybe not so oddly, given his ruggedness—he'd never been around to see Grosstet get killed.

It was a hard pill to swallow. Far harder, naturally, than the delicious plate of pancakes he always came back to. It was simply impossible to get sick of strawberry pancakes. Thus far, the only clear win in his planning of this loop had been the catering. But the verdict was clear.

Eric was the wrong choice for the rescue portion of this mission.

His best attempts were disasters. His worst attempts redefined the term.

He was going to have to find some other way to fix this stubborn loop, and the answer clearly wasn't him.

It also wasn't going to be Grosstet, because in three loops where he'd attempted to reshuffle the teams and convince Jessie to let the haathee take her place, he'd been told in no uncertain terms that she was the essential one on the mission.

The lone attempt where he tried to give Hadrian food poisoning—in an effort to make the rescue an all-Ramsey affair —had been thwarted by a combination of Hadrian's iron stomach, his own squeamishness to try anything more toxic, and a menacingly raised eyebrow.

This was going to be a long haul, and Eric was going to

need to learn the ins and outs of everyone's part if he was going to iron this plan smooth.

———

There was a knock at Jessie's door.

Luckily, she'd reached the point where levi-meditation didn't require a distraction-free environment. And since it wasn't the door chime, it limited the number of visitors to those who didn't know how to use one.

Rolling into a backflip, Jessie dropped to the floor and answered the follow-up knock.

"What?" she demanded when it was her brother on the other side.

He drew a deep breath, and Jessie braced herself against the expected onslaught of nonsense. "I was hoping you could take pity on me and a preemptive apology for my negligence and fill me in on Dad's rescue plan."

Hah. So much for Mr. Ostrich burying his head in the sand and moping about not being wanted on the mission. "Look, you—"

"I know, I as much as told you to leave me out of everything. But I've had a good think, and I know I can handle it."

She folded her arms. "Why the change of heart?" Not just any answer was going to be good enough here. Time was limited. Carl was mere days from execution. If he needed her to be his binky and make his widdle feewings hurt less, he could sit down with his girlfriend and let her do her damned job. He'd be a lot sadder if Carl died because she played along with his nonsense instead of preparing herself, her crew, and her assault team.

"I can contribute." He put up a hand just as she was about

to emphasize that he was *not* coming. Not in Hadrian's place. Not as a third wheel. He was unwelcome. "Any big plan needs someone to poke holes and see if it's still spaceworthy, right?"

"Maybe..." Jessie allowed, though it was one of Dad's big rules of planning.

"I'm a sideways thinker. I'll come up with problems the rest of you won't."

"Such as?" Jessie challenged. Fluffing her ego and using buzzwords was one thing. Eric had words aplenty. But she needed ideas that weren't utter dogshit, or she'd be wasting her time even listening.

"Have you considered that the hoopla around Dad is a big deal for the eyndar? That maybe they're bringing in tourists and VIPs and curious out-of-towners."

"That's part of our disguise plan." At least he'd paid enough attention to know that much.

"What'll that do to pedestrian traffic in the area around the prison? You should have a plan to avoid crowded streets. Memorize buildings you can cut through—shopping centers and stuff—so you can travel against the official flow of pedestrians."

"That... 's a really good idea, actually. All right. You've got your briefing. Lemme just get dressed and meet me in the Briefing Room. I'll bring up the current plan and walk you through it."

Eric looked her up and down. "You're dressed."

That drew a scowl as Jessie snapped the strap of her sports bra at him. "This doesn't count as dressed. Not for a captain."

"If... I had gotten here half an hour earlier, would you have still been in uniform?"

"I... maybe? I don't know. I wasn't looking at a chrono. Why?"

"Nothing. Just curious about timings and missed opportunities. Go ahead. I'll meet you up there."

———

It wasn't often that Eric ventured inside a half-naked spacecraft. Seeing Shuttle 1 with its panels open gave Eric a sensation akin to watching surgery on the holo. Aunt Shoni loved that sort of thing. Those holos made Eric's insides crawl in sympathy; it was similar aside from not having wires and data crystals and whatnot in him. But the H-tech stuff was all hoses full of goo, and that's all humans were when you boiled one down.

But he had to make the effort.

He had to know.

"So, Jomek, old pal, catch me up on what you've been working on these last couple days," Eric announced in advance of sneaking up on the poor mechanic. He'd made Uncle Roddy bang his head so often that he'd been barred from the *Mobius* engine room.

"Much busy hands; not many flappy lips. Your sister's fixing to head out any minute, and I need to finish quickie-quick."

Eric huffed. "Just like Jasmine."

The laugh that followed made Jomek bang his head. He extracted himself still chuckling despite rubbing his forehead. "You know? You're right. I don't mind the big-and-small pair-up, but moderation. Am I right? Every day. Sometimes twice. And that's just the workday. Swear I'm gonna see Treb shriveled like a raisin and her puffed up like a balloon."

Eric cocked his head. "Huh?"

"Never mind. Short answer: I got shit to do, kid. Catch me in an hour."

It occurred to Eric that he didn't need the shuttle here. Just the mechanic. "OK. After, mind talking me through what you found?"

"Hah! Wait... You serious? You look serious."

"I am."

"What's a wizard care about shuttle maintenance?"

"You wouldn't believe how important it is to me."

Jomek shrugged. "Ham is a vegetable, sometimes. Come see me after the mission launches. I'll answer anything you wanna know."

Eric grinned. "That'd be perfect."

―――

Jomek left Trebla's laboratory shaking his head. There ought to have been some minimum criteria before anyone got to call a place a lab. That kid had a tinker shop. Nothing more.

When his datapad hummed, he slipped it out of his trousers with a lower hand, mid-stride. Passing it up to a less-engaged limb, he blew a lip-flapping sigh.

"Course she wants an overhaul. I told her Shuttle 1 needed an overhaul. Did she take me off power relay scrubs?" he asked a door access panel on the way past it. Not programmed to accept voice queries, the panel didn't respond. "No. She lets Trebla keep me in the pump zone while her ride is overdue for a once-over."

But, other than putting in overtime his old bones wouldn't authorize, he didn't have enough time to go off the schedule.

Now, vindicated, he headed down to the hangar to find out what kind of shape Shuttle 1 was in lately.

To his surprise, he found Eric waiting for him. "Hey, Jomek, old buddy!"

"Hiiiiii," Jomek replied warily. Eric spoke to him politely in passing. The kid was the son of an old friend. He'd hardly have considered Eric a "buddy."

The young wizard stepped aside and so as not to impede Jomek's lowering of the shuttle's back ramp. So long as Eric didn't interfere with the mechanic's workday, he was welcome to loiter. Better a wizard loiter than *do* just about anything. Wizards doing things was the beginning of trouble. Hadrian understood that. He did less than anyone aboard, except for maybe Figgy. *That* guy knew how to not do magic—among other things.

Jomek retrieved a set of adapted H-tech tools, sized for laaku and human hands. Logistics had their own, even smaller, set, but the two sizes rarely intermingled in one tool kit other than as a prank. He still remembered the time someone swapped his H-1a wrench for Chinochin's. He tried using it with two fingers for half a morning before abandoning his task to go hunt down the proper tool for hands his size.

"You know," Eric started, always a prelude to some kind of nonsense. "I've been thinking."

"Good stuff, thinking. Better stuff, doing."

"Sure, sure. But I was, in particular, thinking about the fourth left ferrofluidic manifold." He rattled off the part name like he was reading cue cards on the set of a high school holovid production—or was the celebrity endorsing a piece of equipment he'd never seen before in his life.

"OK. Punch my line. What's funny about the fourth left ferrofluidic manifold?" The sooner he got out the far side of the Nonsense Zone, the sooner he could get back to actual work.

Eric cleared his throat and hummed a random note. "The ferrofluidic MAN-i-fold, is almost certainly MUCH-too-old. Please also check on the REG-u-lator, for the port ventral ISO-lator. And if I admit to a FEE-ling, there's something not quite APPEA-ling, about the way Window 3's gasket's SEA-ling."

Jomek scratched his head. "How's that now?"

Eric ticked off on his fingers. "Fourth left ferrofluidic manifold. Regulator on the port ventral isolator. Gasket seal on Window 3. Don't ask how I know. Your profession has its tricks of the trade; so does mine. You can thank me tomorrow when the mission launches and you've been done a full day."

"Ohhh-kaaay. I'll just have a look."

Eric gave a gormless, insouciant grin. "Don't mind me. I'll just wait here until you've at least checked those three. Then I'll run up and grab us lunch. How would three-bird sushi sound?"

"That would—yeah. Definitely. Thanks. I was just thinking I was in the mood for some if I could convince—"

"I already hit up Uom'pe. She said since it was for her favorite customer, she'd do it."

"Was she talking about you, or me?"

"I'll try to remember to ask—if there's a next time."

———

Over the course of perhaps seventy or eighty loops, Eric had come up with his best version of the *Arete's* day.

Finishing his pancakes every morning gave him the strength to run around like a maniac the rest of the day, so he always began a new loop with a healthy breakfast. Afterward, he cleaned up after himself, and while he was back in the kitchen incinerating the residue of syrup and fruit juice from his plate, he hit up Uom'pe for three-bird sushi to butter up Jomek, and to leave out the dash of expired ginger that would cost Jomek half a day back and forth to the washroom.

From there, he raced over to Trebla's lab and swapped the contents of two similar-looking jars of adhesive, which would spark a minor revelation that he wouldn't make on his own until nearly dinnertime.

After that, down to the hangar to direct Jomek to the right parts of Shuttle 1 so that he'd finish ahead of schedule.

After lunch, he knocked on the door to the bridge so he could share a quick hug across the threshold with Charlotte for not setting foot there. Informing her of a pair of Logistics workers gambling on the job would blunt the complaint they were going to file against Eric for bothering them. Later that night, Charlotte *wouldn't* be miffed at him, and he'd get his night off from the Village of Eternity without sitting in a cell.

This was perhaps his favorite of the optimizations he'd come up with. Charlotte ratting him out to Hadrian and sitting out the remainder of a loop in the brig *sucked.*

Jessie giving Eric briefings on the upcoming mission always required feeding her some key insights that Eric wouldn't have come up with in a million years going in blind. The one that seemed to work best was supplying her with an estimate of the time Hadrian took to drop into versus out of astral. For whatever reason, Jessie had never noticed that realspace was easier to find than literally any particular astral depth. It was the difference between hitting a specific pool ball into a pocket you call out and hitting the cue ball with the stick. Of *course* it was extra quick.

Eric supplied five bits of information she needed. First, obviously, was the astral drop thing: that got them into the wastewater pipes instead of the ocean when they emerged into realspace. Big time saver. Then, the back way out of the wastewater plant. Combine that with pointing out the crowds from the festival in the eyndar capital, and Jessie would spot the blockage and backtrack with Hadrian, exiting the wastewater place on the "wrong" side but with foot traffic carrying them toward the prison instead of away from it. The layout of a ground-level shopping center would allow them to exit the crowd and make the final leg of the journey. Lastly, a guy who'd kill Dad, who needed to die.

The morning of day two, Eric would grab a bite to eat with Hadrian, ask about Sparta, and suggest that the killer wizard gather the names of those he was going to murder. Before the big slaughter in the plaza, Hadrian always managed to come away knowing a bunch of names. He was a random element, seeming to kill a new set of eyndar almost every time through, and Eric managed to assemble a pretty solid working list of eyndar on duty that day.

He had pointers for Lisa's presentation.

There were two games of cards with Logistics, so they wouldn't know Eric was the one who turned them in.

And of course, there was the favor to keep Hadrian from being in a foul mood that seemed to grow slightly worse every loop until Eric had fixed it.

—

Sparta rocked and heaved, and Mort took his turn lying on his back while the pair discussed the utter mundanities of the galaxy as they made love.

She was a vision of Hellenistic beauty. Alexandros of Antioch couldn't have sculpted her better. Oh, he realized that his opinion might have carried little weight in the artistic galaxy, but Mort couldn't think of a single artist he'd ever met who wasn't a complete pushover.

He muttered responses to her opinions on tesud cuisine as his mind and fingers both wandered the more interesting curves of her body. Mort traced her as if he wished to finger paint her from memory later. Every inch of flesh. Every little piercing that decorated her. He slid his hand over bracelets and under necklaces. He fiddled and fidgeted and teased.

Suddenly, Sparta stiffened head to toe, and not in the way he was trying for. Something was the matter.

"If you need me to move my fingers, I can certainly—"

Head thrown back, a plaintive wail escaped Sparta's gaping mouth. She eased off pinning Mort's shoulders to the bed and clutched the sides of her head.

Sitting up awkwardly, Mort took her gingerly by the waist and steadied her.

"Magic... visions... make it stop."

Mort immediately clamped down, and Sparta gasped in relief. But she still had the look of a novice to the Order who'd just taken his palm off the burning cauldron in the great hall and still not finished regretting taking that bet.

"Can... Is... What can I do here?" Suggesting that finishing might help would have sounded self-serving at the moment.

"*Eenok tra'raal*," Sparta replied.

"When did you start learning eyndar?"

"I haven't."

"Then how'd you ask me to state my business in butchered eyndar?"

From the wall, there was a creak, a scrape of ceramic on metal, and the flopping slap of a vent being allowed to fall closed.

An aroma wafted to the bed.

"That smell..." Sparta's eyes glazed over. She fluttered a hand toward it. As she was bereft of magic herself, at the moment, Mort did the honors of levitating a teacup toward the bed. There had better be a good explanation for that intrusion, otherwise the crew were going to have to get used to seeing some blue-furred rodents running around the ship.

Sparta accepted the beverage and lifted it to her nose.

"Ahh." She took a sip. "Oh, even better. This will do splendidly."

"What is it? Smells are still hit or miss with this nose."

"C-K tea."

"Never heard of it. Is it helping?"

Sparta took a longer sip, tipping back what must have been still near boiling with just the faintest wince. "It will in short order. It's chamomile and ketamine. An old recipe for calming visions."

———

Time and again, Eric found himself in the hangar, waiting for the loop where Jessie and Hadrian would deliver Dad safe and sound—or at least intact and revivable. At this point, Eric wasn't inclined to be picky. Harmony fished in the shallow afterlife with a net.

But it didn't seem to be in the cards.

Time and again, Dad came back in the shuttle past the point of no return.

Sometimes the blaster hole was in a different spot. Clean shot to the heart. Right through the skull. Belly. Lung. Occasionally there was a second shot, usually a shoulder or leg. After a while, Eric just avoided looking.

Once in a while, the shuttle didn't return at all. The loop just reset without the closure of seeing the failure in person.

In a realization that Eric could only describe as both sweet and noble, Shuttle 1 never returned without Jessie, Hadrian, and Dad all present.

Eric took to watching the carnage from the four newsfeeds in the holovid theater. But the information was so consistently misleading, the footage so distant and manipulated by science, and both Hadrian and Jessie protected from view by magic that he learned next to nothing.

This time, he waited by the lift with a thermal mug in hand.

He watched the spot where Shuttle 1 had departed just moments ago and didn't take his eyes off the spot where it had been parked. When the lift doors opened, he merely held out the mug until it was retrieved.

"They're gone?" Sparta asked.

"How come you never want to say goodbye?"

"How can I?" she asked, taking a sip from the mug. "I never told him what I saw. Some of it blurted out in a moment of... well, by accident at any rate. But nothing revelatory. Nothing that would divert his course. I can't see Hadrian's future, but I can catch glimpses of it, like reflections in a mirror when his fate is caught up in someone else's whose I can view. And if I try to explain it—"

"He kills me to end the loop. It's happened three times, now. Never works. Even when I explain that it won't, he tells me it serves me right."

"It does, you know. Serve you right."

"I'm really sorry. I had no idea it would do this to you."

"You had no Earthly idea what it would do. No point denying it. These fortunate clods all around us are blissful in their ignorance. Actors in a popular Broadway play that simply won't end its run. Same show, night after night."

"The loop's about two days."

"Believe me. I know."

"Do you ever see anything that... you know... maybe you could share with *me* that might help end this?"

"Of your own volition, you might be able to break the loop without satisfying it. Using chronomancy a second time. I doubt Hadrian could compel you, or I'd have suggested it."

"You did. That was one of the three times."

Sparta harrumphed softly and sipped her tea. "See? I don't have perfect recall. It's more like a box of archival news clippings dumped across a table."

"Any advice at all? Doesn't have to be from visions. You're... well, I can convince Grosstet I'm in a time loop, and two superstitious ratatoret. Uom'pe humors me. Trebla plays along as a thought experiment before eventually telling me I'm crazy. And Figgy just can't get sober enough at any time in the loop to offer useful guidance. You're really the only one who'll both believe me and be of any help—and not murder me," he added.

"Without compiling a list of variables, you seem to have honed your preparations of the rescue team to a razor's edge. I'm not sure how much you can improve upon this plan."

"I know... Hadrian and Jessie just get there too late, and they won't accept being rushed. I can steal the shuttle and go with Grosstet, and we get there in plenty of time, but the two of us are a disaster. We're not sneaky *at all*, and I can't just... well, I'm not Hadrian. I can't go around making scary newsfeeds for the whole galaxy."

"Those are the only plans you've tried?"

"Jessie won't step back and let Hadrian go with Grosstet. He's the better pilot, even if only for his own shuttle. I think the two of them could manage it, but without hurting Jessie, I don't see how I could pull it off."

"Think farther outside the box, then. What about discovering a way to contact your Aunt Jamie?"

"Thought of that. No one even knows where to start. She's good and hidden."

"What about shanghaiing your sister with Grosstet."

"He won't do it. And he's too stubborn to *make* do it. I can only even get him to come along by making him feel like a hero."

"Well, we're doomed then. Eternity of struggles and failure for your lack of imagination." Sparta took a long drink from the tea Eric had brought her. He didn't even know how she was standing. Two sips of that stuff, and he'd been petting unicorns and drifting through the ship with his toes dragging behind him.

But she had a point. If the perfect implementation of the Hadrian and Jessie rescue plan wasn't ever going to work, he needed a new baseline to start from. But somehow, the stealth mission with a wizard and a pilot seemed just... right.

Eric couldn't explain *why* it felt right, but he trusted the feeling.

If only he'd gotten his pilot's license as a teenager. Mom and Dad had both offered to teach him, but Uncle Enzio warned that, while it was possible, it would make him both a bad pilot *and* a bad wizard, and a younger Eric Ramsey wasn't willing to be bad at *everything* he ever did.

Going solo, assuming he could fly a shuttle, Eric felt confident that he could sneak his way to the eyndar military prison, free Dad, and get back. Heck, *flying* back would be easy. They could stay in astral for days, if need be, until Dad was in fit shape to fly Shuttle 1 himself. Or talk Eric through it.

If only Eric knew how to fly.

He snorted in amusement at the notion.

"Something funny?"

"Oh, you just got me thinking. If only wizards could fly. I'd do the whole thing myself. Or at least try. I'm not sure it's the kind of thing that trial and error can get you, though. Maybe a few thousand loops, I could pick up enough to make a go of it."

"God..." Sparta tilted back the mug and chugged. She gasped, eyes barely focusing. "You know, Hadrian mentioned once that two of his apprentices were pilots of a sort. You miss class that day?"

"He got me young," Eric explained. "Aunt Esper and Aunt... Aunt Tiffany. They had pilot's licenses before they ever learned magic. Aunt Esper is retired, basically. In her day, I bet she could have done it. But Aunt Tiffany..."

"The cheerless psychopath with the fashion sense of a street urchin?"

"Oh. I didn't know you knew her."

"We've been introduced. When Hadrian was still upholding the pretense of being an adviser to Emperor Khosrau, she was there one time, and I took my measure of her —and vice versa."

Eric cocked his head. "You don't sound like you liked her."

"I believe that woman makes a special effort to be disliked."

"She's an old family friend," Eric argued. Sure, maybe they'd played that card before, but Eric wasn't above rummaging around the discard pile like it was a game of Go Fish.

"She works for Emperor Khosrau. Personally."

Eric shook his head. "Who cares. She's perfect. She's *just* who we need."

Shuttle 1 didn't return from this particular loop. But it was the last time that was going to matter.

A fork fell with a clatter that rang through the dining lounge.

IT ALL STARTS HERE

Eric ate his pancakes slowly, mind turning over an all-new problem. A zillionty tasks he'd lined up, practiced, and set up like precarious dominoes lay strewn about the ship, unattended to. As the opportunity for each went by the wayside... As Eric cleaned up dishes without asking Uom'pe for a favor... As Trebla went about fumbling with his glue selections and Jomek went to work checking every part of Shuttle 1 when most of it was perfectly fine... As Jessie missed glaring errors in her rescue planning...

... Eric tried to figure out how he was going to contact Aunt Tiffany to ask a favor.

Of course, he still snagged Tippitak on the side and asked if she could get her brother-in-law to brew up some C-K tea and send it to Hadrian and Sparta's room. He owed Sparta that much.

But the rest of this loop was heading into a decaying orbit that he wasn't going to bother averting.

Jessie was no help as his first stop on the Tiffany Comm ID Scavenger Hunt.

"We're on comm lockdown. No unauthorized comms in or out. We're in last-minute planning mode, and we can't afford distractions."

"Yeah, but can't you authorize—?"

"Request denied."

Trebla was willing to cough up the ID on the condition that Eric not use it until the comm blackout ended. Eric felt bad when he whammied Trebla and got him to bypass the comm system and worse when it turned out that the ID was outdated and no longer in use.

Harmony refused to help him. Three different loops. Three different approaches. Same "leave her out of this" wall of stony willpower. Eric couldn't even whammy an ID out of her. Too much science on the brain.

He went back to whammying Trebla loop after loop and using his access to the wider galaxy to poll friends and family.

Using some of the few comm IDs he'd memorized, Eric

used the comm panel in his bedroom while Charlotte was working and contacted everyone he could think of who might help.

Aunt Esper answered right away, but she didn't like the idea. "*I could give you a comm ID, but it's old. She doesn't keep one for long nowadays. Whatever you want to talk to her about, I'd recommend against it.*"

"Let's say, for the sake of argument, I just want to catch up on old times."

"*Let's also just say, for the sake of argument, that you didn't inherit the liar's gene from your father. You want to enlist her help in a crazed scheme to rescue your father, don't you?*"

"For the sake of argument, what if I did?"

"*Then, for the sake of argument, I'd tell you you're better off without her help. Eric, I know this is hard for you to comprehend, but the galaxy doesn't revolve around you. And while it might appear that it's presently revolving around Carl, rest assured that, much as I grieve for him, there's not much to be done. War with the Eyndar Empire is almost inevitable at this point. Earth won't act rashly in the build-up to that. And Tiffany works directly for Khosrau, as much as she claims to still be a librarian. What Earth wants is what Khosrau wants.*"

"Could you just give me the ID and let me try?" Eric begged.

"*For your own good, no.*"

Two more loops trying, and Eric realized Aunt Esper wasn't weak-willed enough to waver.

His next avenue was Aunt Yomin.

"*You holdin' up OK, sugar? I know you ain't gone commin' me for nothing, ya? Don't think I ain't been doin' all I can for your father.*"

"What about a current comm ID for Aunt Tiffany?"

Aunt Yomin scoffed. *"Dat one, she's more trouble than she be worth."*

"You couldn't find one, then?"

Aunt Yomin's scowl yelled while her voice grew quiet. *"Nah. She gets found when she wants ta be found. And right about now, she don't want nothing ta do with dis. Or me. Or you."*

"All right. Thanks." Eric ended the comm with magic, and it rendered the unit useless for over an hour.

That gave him time to think. To plan. Not that he didn't have all the time in the universe. Actually, *ending* his infinite surplus of time was the end goal here. Even if saving Dad's life hadn't been the primary motivator going into the time loop, he really *did* need to escape it at some point.

Madness lay in his distant future, thousands—or millions—of loops from now. And once madness set in, there would be no escape.

Examining his own actions of late, it was hard to argue that Eric wasn't *completely* not-mad. He'd already started providing tea, but he'd yet to start wearing funny hats. And perhaps it was that little *touch* of madness that got him to look in unusual ways and unusual places for his answers.

He swiped Jessie's datapad and got Grosstet to hack into it. Grosstet was a sucker for the heroism line and could be convinced of nearly any course of action if Eric psyched him up with a good pep rally.

But Jessie's ID was outdated, too.

The *Arete's* computer could find the home addresses of Earth Navy admirals, but it didn't know Aunt Tiffany even existed.

Makket's old criminal cronies couldn't track down an ID.

Uom'pe's grandchildren were no help.

Lisa's mercenary contacts turned up nothing.

Lorenzo barely knew who Eric was even talking about.

Mindy and Daphne were less than polite every time Eric tried to enlist their help; they were both so invested in Dad's rescue planning that he couldn't really even be mad.

In the end, it was the least likely resource that turned out to be his connection.

Xrista.

Getting volunteer time babysitting was easy, and she shared her datapad freely.

Thanks to a paranoid mom, the list of emergency contacts in the datapad read like a family reunion. She had everyone in there.

Aunt Esper

Aunt Karen

Two personal assistants

Five Harmony Bay directors

Mom

Dad

A guy named Hector Hectare

Kubu and his wife

All Harmony's sisters

Several high-ranking members of the Martian Exile Government

A scattering of Hollyworld agents

Jessie

Eric was almost offended not showing up anywhere before remembering that he didn't have a comm ID.

Everyone was in there. Labeled, which was the only reason Eric knew who half of them even were, and cataloged, sorted in a priority Eric couldn't decipher.

But in there, nestled among the rest, with a tag that read "Very Big, REAL, Emergencies," was Aunt Tiffany.

Eric memorized the ID and tried it the following loop.

It worked.

"*Eric? Oh, fuck the fuck right fucking off. Who gave you this ID?*"

Thinking ahead, he asked, "What would be an acceptable answer to that question?"

"*Look, I don't care what you think you're doing. I'm waiting on orders, and I don't take a whole lot of orders. Got it? I'm in no mood for whatever shit you're up to. Given the newsfeeds, you want me involved in something in eyndar space. Some number of executions between five and seven?*"

"Yes."

"*Cram it, time boy. Your old man's had the Grim Reaper's comm ID blocked for longer than I've known him. Either his number is up or he's going to slip through again like a sock in the laundry.*"

"He won't," Eric assured her. "We need to help him, and I can't do it without you."

"*Galli's Scissors, you little asshole! You did it, didn't you? I've had the worst déjà vu this morning. You fucked with time to save Carl, didn't you?*"

"You don't get out of the time loop without helping me." Eric hated playing hardball, but it was also the truth.

"*You made this mess. You can get out of it.*"

The comm ended abruptly.

Ten subsequent loops didn't improve the conversation any. One even went so badly that Aunt Tiffany ratted him out to Hadrian, who killed Eric for, as best he could remember it, the fourth time.

Despondent, Eric allowed five more loops to play out as they saw fit, not even bothering to attend the finale of each. But all ended the same.

A fork fell with a clatter that rang through the dining lounge.

WORDS THAT HURT YOU / 83

IT ALL STARTS HERE

Tiffany was the answer.

As Eric ate his umpteenth plate of the same strawberry pancakes, he pondered the question he had to ask and that he'd yet to pose.

Eric had whammied Trebla so many times by now that the poor guy was probably getting afterimages of the insides of Eric's eyeballs. It had become his first stop after breakfast, slipping in and out of Trebla's quarters before Jasmine's comm distracted him. He could only hope that on the loop that finally broke Eric free with Dad safe that Trebla recovered properly.

Technically... *technically* it would only have happened once. But repeatedly fiddling with someone's brain was reportedly dangerous. First to the victim, for somewhat obvious reasons. Secondly, to the perpetrator, because that was exactly the sort of thing that got inquisitors and librarians sniffing around for dark wizards.

Eric wasn't a dark wizard, but he admitted to a potential vibe that might get him in trouble one of these days.

Still, none of that mattered until the far side of the loop, and Eric could foresee so many loops yet ahead of him.

Once Trebla had bid him yet another groggy goodbye, only to be perked up again by thoughts of an upcoming tryst, Eric scampered back to his quarters. With Charlotte in the middle of a long shift and the Logistics guys in the vents keeping well clear of his room without a darned good reason, Eric decided to apply some treason to his plan.

He had a recipe for success in mind, and the treasoning was his seasoning.

His first comm was voice only. *"Hello, Boston Convocation Outreach Center, how may I help you?"*

"I'm a wizard in null space with important information about the starship *Arete*. Who can I speak with?"

"The what!? You mean that rogue alien starship from beyond the known galaxy?"

There were some factual inaccuracies there that Eric was willing to brush past for the sake of expediency. "Yes. But I only want to speak to someone important about it. Who's the most important person you're authorized to pass me along to?"

"H-h-hold on," the liaison stammered in a panic. *"Let me get my supervisor."*

"No rush. I have all day. But the intel will only get older the longer you take."

A gruff, officious voice returned to the comm. *"Who the blazes is this?"*

In for a penny, in for a terra, as they say. "I'm Eric Ramsey, Order of Chronos."

"There's no such order."

"I haven't founded it yet," Eric snapped, doing his best Uncle Enzio impression. "But cut to the chase, I'm aboard the starship *Arete*, I know where it is, and I'm willing to share that information for the low, low price of speaking with the highest-ranking person you're authorized to pass the buck to."

"How can I know you're not some kook looking to bother someone?"

"I'm being up front about it: I plan to bother someone. Your boss's boss, if you can manage that, your boss if you can't. Make me someone else's problem."

"If you're a fraud, I'll be the one to suffer. Not you. Prove you know something of value."

"I'm sorry. I didn't catch your name. To whom am I speaking?"

"*I am Elroy van Buren, Order of Hermes.*"

Crap. Order of Hermes? This guy may as well have been another liaison. Messenger wizards had access to just about anyone but authority over practically no one. Still, Eric had to start somewhere. And he had a bit of Dad in him, didn't he? Mom always insisted when people questioned his parentage.

"Van Buren? I think I might have attended college with your son. What was his name... Marty?" It was the first name to pop into Eric's head, and a wrong guess didn't matter. "I think we bowled together."

"*My* daughter, *Marcia, was a debater. Good day, you fraud.*" There was a long pause, but the comm panel didn't shut off. Eric knew what getting hung up on looked like, and it wasn't this. The same voice, more distant, echoed from the screen. "*What do you mean it's still on? Off is your job, not mine... Yes, I want it off! I bid that miscreant good day, which you should have—*"

There. The screen was dark.

Eric huffed a sigh. It was good work for one loop.

He fiddled with a few other variables for the rest of day one and all of day two, mentally replaying the conversation over and over so he wouldn't forget, and spent the rest of his time making the loop as enjoyable as possible, knowing the gut punch waiting for him at the end.

But blissfully, eventually, it ended.

A fork fell with a clatter that rang through the dining lounge.

IT ALL STARTS HERE

⊏⊐

"*I am Elroy van Buren, Order of Hermes.*"

Eric had managed to steer his way through the same

conversations after two tries. Last loop, he'd fumbled the timing and gotten a different liaison. Today, he'd just asked for a transfer based on a description of the first liaison's voice and was transferred to one Cody Pips. Cody, when pressed, had handed him off to Elroy again.

This time, Eric knew just what to say.

"Van Buren? I knew a Marcia van Buren back in college. Any relation? I think we debated together."

"*Why yes. My daughter debated for Yale. But Eric Ramsey is an Oxford alumnus.*"

"Yeah. I met her at a meet. Anyway, I'm looking for someone to make a plea deal. Exchange location intelligence on the starship *Arete* for someone to listen to my side of the story."

"*I'm listening, presently.*"

"Don't take this the wrong way, but I'd like someone higher up the chain of command. Say 'hi' to Marcia for me, and no hard feelings. But I'd like someone to put me through to the Inquisitors' Office."

This time, Eric was able to move one step up the ladder.

But over in the Inquisitors' Office, Eric was once again stonewalled. They believed him. He got to speak to the Assistant Chief Inquisitor, if not the Chief herself.

"*No, we will not make any considerations for your offer of inconsequential knowledge. The location of the starship* Arete *is not currently a priority of the Inquisition. If you wish to turn yourself in, by all means, do so. Otherwise, you are no concern of mine.*"

Well, that set Eric back a few loops.

But after a few errant attempts that got him disconnected on repeatedly, he stumbled onto another avenue.

"Van Buren? I knew a Marcia van Buren back in college. Any relation?" The name was a password. "I think we debated against one another."

"*Why yes. My daughter debated for Yale. I didn't realize you represented Oxford.*"

"Yeah. I didn't stick with it. Anyway, I'm looking for someone to make a bargain. I have knowledge of chronomancy that belongs in the Library of the Plundered Tomes."

"*What kind of knowledge?*"

"Don't take this the wrong way, but I'd like someone higher up the chain of command. Say 'hi' to Marcia for me, and no hard feelings." The no hard feelings were going to cover the deception, theoretically, but Eric had never gotten far enough to witness any aftermath of his lie. "But I'd like someone to put me through to a librarian."

There was an extended wait. Eric fidgeted but didn't give up. Inquisitors were plentiful, busybody bureaucrats. They lived for reports and acting on them. As much as *certain* librarians made it seem otherwise, the care and study of books was the primary function of the Library of the Plundered Tomes.

"*Someone said you were Eric Ramsey.*" The voice was gruff yet wimpy. It conjured memories of a shopping center Santa Claus that smelled of bourbon. "*I am Wizard Galantix, Special Assistant Scribe of the Guardian of the Plundered Tomes.*"

"That someone was correct. I've got new revelations that I'd like to arrange delivery of."

"*Drop them at your nearest Liaison's Office or Outreach Center with instructions that originals must be delivered to Boston unopened, unviewed, undisturbed.*"

"Not good enough. I need the services of a *top* acquisitions librarian."

"*Believe me, you don't want that kind of attention. Just submit whatever documents you've got, and stop writing more!*"

"Excuse me, I think I need to speak to your superior."

"*Hah! Bad enough you had them drag me in front of this*

infernal speaking window. I'm not going to summon Azrael Copperfield on a child's whim."

"Very well. Thank you for your time." That was progress enough for one loop.

Next loop, Eric didn't even bother with van Buren.

———

As soon as the first liaison answered his comm, Eric pulled out the new ace up his sleeve.

"Hello, Boston Convocation Outreach Center, how may I help you?"

"Yes, I was speaking with Wizard Galantix, and we got disconnected when he tried to transfer me to Azrael Copperfield."

"You... were speaking to the Special Assistant Scribe of the Guardian of the Plundered Tomes?"

"Yes, this is Dark Wizard Eric Ramsey, and I need to be speaking to Councilor Azrael Copperfield, and I imagine he's going to be cross if I'm not prompt getting this resolved. Please, this isn't the time to be awestruck."

"I'm not awestruck! I'm... hold on a second, and I'll get the connection established."

There was, perhaps, a story taking place in the background, halfway across the galaxy as identities were confirmed, lies hastily not questioned, and librarians bothered. Because when the pause ended, Eric heard a voice that hadn't struck his ears since his expulsion.

"So, you've managed to contact me directly, Wizard Eric. To what end, I wonder."

"I need Tiffany Bell's services, and she works for you."

A mocking, sardonic laugh preceded Azrael's reply. *"Of all the impudence!"*

The comm ended. No one Eric contacted subsequently was willing to give him so much as a connection to a high-ranking liaison after that.

Next loop, Eric attempted a different approach.

"*So, you've managed to contact me directly, Wizard Eric. To what end, I wonder.*"

"I have new chronomancy literature and I'm willing to bargain."

"*Your excremental scribblings barely warranted archiving in the first place. It's the only reason you're not already dead.*"

The comm ended.

Eric scowled and went about thinking over tactics ahead of his next loop.

"*So, you've managed to contact me directly, Wizard Eric. To what end, I wonder.*"

"Mordecai The Brown is alive, and I know where you can find him."

There was a long pause. "*You're bluffing.*"

"Am not!"

"*I knew Mordecai The Brown, and you, young rapscallion, are no acquaintance of his. He died before you were born.*"

The comm ended. Eric spent several loops pestering Hadrian piecemeal about the habits of Azrael Copperfield.

———

"*So, you've managed to contact me directly, Wizard Eric. To what end, I wonder.*"

"I know you once aided and abetted Mordecai The Brown in a grand deception that's the only reason you kept your job in the early days as Guardian of the Plundered Tomes."

"*I don't know with whom you've been gossiping, but you are misinformed. Any attempts to blackmail me or malign me*" *publicly with this falsehood will result in mockery and scorn not even worthy of reprisal."*

The comm ended. Eric spent dozens of loops largely hanging around with Hadrian, just the two of them. With the cat out of the bag with so many other people, and Hadrian on the verge of confessing his true identity far and wide, Eric asked a million questions and studied not just the responses but the mannerisms. And, after a few hiccups, managed to do it without raising the wizard's ire—or suspicions.

"So, you've managed to contact me directly, Wizard Eric. To what end, I wonder."

"Are you alone?"

"This conversation is private, if that's what you're getting at."

Eric issued a harrumph that had taken a good deal of practice to get right. "Good. I'm Mordecai The Brown, and I'm calling in a very, very old favor."

He hadn't tried to fake the voice. The manner of speech did the trick.

"No..." Despite the denial, the Guardian of the Plundered Tomes was shaken.

"Yes."

"A ruse. You can't possibly be him."

"Try me. I've been body-hopping, mind to mind. You saw what I wanted you to see. I was in Esper Richelieu's mind when you inspected her memories. I took over others. I was Enzio Stiles for a long while. But recently I've taken a liking to this body. Too bad it didn't come with the knowledge of time travel I was after. But I'm young again. And debts only gather interest with age."

Eric was particularly proud of working that last bit in. It might not have proved that he *was* Mort, but it certainly hinted that he knew him well. And Eric, young as he was, should never have met the man.

"This is a trick. A good one, I admit. I don't know how you've managed to pull it off, but Mordecai The Brown is dead!"

Suddenly, Eric felt he was losing his grip on the situation. This particular shade of anger and pique preceded being unceremoniously disconnected from the comm.

"Fine, I'm not Mordecai The Brown. You're caught up in my time loop, and I'll keep getting better and better at this ruse the longer I practice it. But know that every new loop is a new chance, however small, of shattering reality with you inside it."

"FOOL! We gave you every chance to mend your ways. Give up magic. Even just giving up on your stupid pretensions of chronomancy. And yet you still pursued it! What is it you want of me?"

"I need to speak with Emperor Khosrau. It's urgent, and he's going to want to hear from me. And if you tell me the approach you're planning to take, I'll inform you next loop if it doesn't work."

"You... you... reckless, arrogant little monster. There's a boulder in Hades with your name on it for this hubris."

"I'll take that as a yes."

There was a feral snarl from the voice-only connection that Eric could nonetheless pair with a vivid sneer. *"I shall approach the emperor with a promise that he will speak with a chronomancer willing to strike a bargain for his services. Will that suffice?"*

Just to mess with Azrael and keep him off guard, Eric replied. "Nah. You tried that last time."

This was it.

Eric's do or die scenario was coming to fruition. From all that he'd been able to gather from Hadrian (who was actually Mort), Emperor Khosrau Blackstone (who was actually Hadrian) had gained a great deal of power and influence with the universe simply thanks to the fear and adulation he garnered from his inherited position.

Before, Old Hadrian (now known as Khosrau) wasn't a match for Eric. Now, maybe he was on equal terms with his predecessor. If anyone could break free of the time loop and wreak vengeance for Eric having started it, it would be the emperor of all humanity (minus Mars and independents and people who chose to live in the League of Independent Planets).

"*I trust that all is secure on your end?*" Khosrau asked, but it was more of a demand for assurance.

"Heh. It's your end I'd be worried about," Eric replied, remaining in character as Mort.

"*So, you took over the Ramsey kid? Was the burden of the Brown name so great that you'd rather be a notorious chronomancer?*"

"I'm not contacting you to talk about that. I have a favor to ask."

"*A favor? You had all the power in the galaxy, and you didn't want it. You can't beg favors like I owe you anything. I took a job you couldn't just abandon. If anything, you owe me for your freedom.*"

"That's one opinion. But this one's minor, so you'll hear me out." Eric couldn't imagine actually saying that as himself. Only paying attention to Mort's speech pattern allowed him to even pretend to be that rude. "I need to borrow the services of Tiffany Bell."

Khosrau scoffed. "Minor, you say. Oh, just let me divert the

Plundered Tomes' most formidable acquisitions librarian. Too lazy to do your own killings, or have you just gone soft?"

Puzzling. Eric couldn't believe anyone spoke to Mort like this. At least, not while actually *knowing* it was Mort. Maybe the emperor was on to the ruse. Otherwise, there were candles that could expect a longer lifespan.

In fact, that gave him an idea.

"I wouldn't be so quick to dismiss my request."

"*Consider it dismissed. I already know why you'd want her. That body's father. Odd way to repay a friendship. But I won't judge. But if you want that boy's father off the eyndar homeworld, do it yourself. He may be an amiable fool, but he is, ultimately, merely a fool.*"

"You think you can just blow me off? With no consequences? Well, I—"

"*Yes,*" Khosrau cut in. "*I think exactly that. Enjoy your freedom, Eric, or Hadrian, or whatever you'd like to be called. The price was paid for it. No refunds. No debts outstanding. Good day.*"

The comm went silent.

Darn.

Of course, Eric wasn't going to be able to take "no" for an answer.

OK. Maybe he *was* going to take it. There wasn't a lot of choice. But he planned to keep asking, loop after loop, as long as it took.

⸺

"*So, you took over the Ramsey kid? Was the burden of the Brown name so great that you'd rather be a notorious chronomancer?*"

Eric tried a different response. "That's neither here nor there. Look, I'm contacting you with a bargain in mind."

"*What could you* possibly *offer me that I don't already have?
I command the grandest star navy in the cosmos. The wealth of
entire planets is at my disposal. This afternoon, I will pick out
four new additions to my harem. I can rule for a century and
father a thousand heirs. Maybe this wasn't your dream, but I
have all that any simple wizard could wish for.*"

That *was* a pretty good point. None of that sounded like
Eric's cup of tea. But it did fit with what a lot of wizards
claimed to desire. Wealth. Power. Sexual partners.

How would *Mort* convince his successor?

Mortishly, no doubt. "Be a shame if that were all to come
crumbling down around your ears. Or... should I say... *burn*
down around you."

"*Are you really daring to* threaten *me?*"

"I'd assumed you'd figure that out without needing to be
told." OK. There was some fun in being Mort. He could just
say mean things that popped into his head without realizing
that he'd be a jerk and then choosing something nicer.

"*I've not been idle since taking this position. Vincente has
been incredibly forthcoming about your mannerisms, your
moods, your strengths, and yes, even your weaknesses. You
won't get near me. You can't assail my power even if you did.
Whatever you want from me, you can't have it. If you attempt
to subvert me in any way, you know the resources at my
disposal.*"

Now probably wasn't the best time to mention needing
Aunt Tiffany's help. Especially since that was, presumably, the
resource Khosrau referred to.

Well, shoot. This loop was ruined already. Eric broke
character. "What if I said I really *was* just Eric and I was faking
being Mort to get you to take my comm?"

"*Merlin's beard, man. Have some self-respect.*"

The comm went silent.

Eric headed back to the dining lounge for a good, long ice-cream think.

Ten more loops passed.

Or was it twelve?

Eric had honestly lost count. He missed the Village of Eternity, where Uriela would have been able to track that sort of minutiae on his behalf. But until he escaped the loop, there was no telling the damage he'd do to his mind trying to access it. Even trying to peek gave him a headache the likes of which ended any follow-up attempts.

Each time though, he hung around with Mort as Hadrian, trying to glean more insights about Hadrian as Khosrau. Eric had never been great at presents, and negotiations were basically just gift-giving with strings attached in both directions.

"Did he seem to have any hobbies?" Eric asked as he shared beers with Hadrian in a disused lounge with a decent view of the stars.

Hadrian shook his head. "Not before we swapped. Not near as I could tell, anyway. His whole life was centered around some perceived grievance against his father. Didn't care to get the details out of him. Plenty of grievance with that father of his myself." Hadrian chuckled. "I suppose that's the most natural part playing this role. I can tell Cedric to fuck off and make it sound like I mean it."

"Any guesses as to what might have happened? Speculation. Humor me." Eric drank and listened.

"Don't know what point it was that rat bastard left his wife and kid, but Cedric didn't leave his family well off. That scientist wife of his had to raise a wizard with little guidance. Amazing the boy turned out magical at all. Well, maybe not *amazing*. He's a Brown, after all. But where Cedric had the best of everything but fathers, Hadrian was forced to get by with table scraps and pull himself up by the shirt collar."

"Good thing he learned levitation. Go on..."

"I mean, that's what there is to it. Must have been when Hadrian was old enough to remember it. Can't hate a fellow that hard without knowing him. Ceddie was young enough that he hated a concept of me, not actually me." Hadrian was lifting his beer to his lips when suddenly he scrunched his whole face. "How is it that you got me blathering like an old man about the past?"

"We just sort of stumbled into it," Eric replied lamely.

"You're just unusually personable today."

Eric shrugged mid-chug of his own beer, which he was turning to water with each swallow. In truth, it had taken countless loops to catch Hadrian in an unguarded moment. He was the finickiest member of the crew, most prone to sudden changes in behavior loop to loop, but the C-K tea for Sparta made her symptoms more consistent each time through and, by extension, Hadrian's actions.

Tomorrow, Eric would alter the conversation slightly, get different stories, and continue learning what made Emperor Khosrau tick.

And, in a strange symbiosis, learning from Khosrau just how others perceived Mordecai The Brown.

"I trust that all is secure on your end?" Khosrau asked, same as every time.

"Probably," Eric replied. "Not really my department."

He could hear the scowl through the voice-only comm. *"You're not Hadrian. Who is this?"*

"I'm Eric. You're Hadrian. Let's be clear about who's who. You're the guy with the manpower—womanpower, in this case. I'm the guy who can alter time."

"How dare you disturb me under false preten—alter what, now? You can jump ahead in time, nothing more."

"That was before. I mean, the nice librarians kept telling me what would happen to me if I kept up trying to figure out real time travel—the good backward kind—and I have. But this is a time loop. You're trapped in it with me."

"So, extortion, is it?"

"No. A straight-up trade of services. I need your help to save my father. I've tried. I can't get the right people to the eyndar homeworld in time to rescue him. Wrong skills. Wrong people. You have the right librarian for the job. And I can make it worth your while."

A silence crystallized with frost. *"I'm listening."*

"How would you like to go back and have another chance? Track down your father. Make him pay for leaving you."

"Why would you think that would matter to me?"

"Because this is a time loop. And you'd have ended the comm by now if I didn't have your complete attention."

"I'm still not convinced your word is good."

Eric sighed. "Fine. Tell me something, something innocuous but utterly convincing that I could say that you'd know in an instant I could only have gotten from you."

"What would that prove?"

"This time? Nothing. Next time, you'll believe me."

Eric scowled as he listened.

The next loop, the conversation tracked exactly up until...

"I'm still not convinced your word is good."

"You were on the fence about Euphrates MacGowan, but

she's not Khosrau's cousin, she'd have been Hadrian's. You're willing to let blood be blood if she looks as good without clothes when you inspect her later today."

"*I had not even told Vincente... So, you did it. You managed to go back in time.*"

"The loop resets when my father dies and can't be saved by dark medicine. If someone gets him off the eyndar homeworld, the loop will break, and I'll owe you the biggest favor."

"*I see. And you presuppose that Tiffany Bell can carry out this rescue?*"

"Our team is going to arrive in about thirty hours from now, and that's way too late. In previous loops I've made it to the homeworld in less than six, but I can't be sneaky enough to avoid a fight with the whole capital city. In your body, Mort can massacre the whole city for killing Dad, so I think Aunt Tiffany might be able to manage. Sneaky is probably the way to go if you can pass that along. I've talked to Tiffany directly in previous loops. Her only concern was that she works for you, not me. If you tell her to do it, I think it'll get done. And if she fails, make sure she tells me what went wrong so we can learn better for next time."

"*You really have been looping time, haven't you?*"

"Yeah."

"*How many times has it been? How many times have we had some version of this same conversation?*"

"I've lost count of both tallies."

"*A guess, then.*"

"A few hundred. Maybe a thousand loops by now? With you, a couple dozen, at most. It took a long time for me to figure out the right plan. I think we're close. We can do this."

"*All for that buffoon of a father of yours?*"

"I'd do anything to save him. So would Jessie. So would Mort. They don't know about the loop yet. Not in this loop.

Neither of them takes it well when they find out. I'd appreciate it if you didn't try to contact them until Dad's safe."

"*Hmm... You suggest an interesting opportunity. The risk of failure seems minimal, and apparently there is no choice, ultimately, except success.*"

"That's the spirit."

"*As for what I desire in return...*"

"You name it. It's yours. Just hurry. I don't know how long it'll take Aunt Tiffany to do all her rescuing. I can talk her through the preparation the *Arete* crew have been doing, and—"

"*My own intelligence vastly surpasses that of the starship Arete's, I have no doubt. Librarian Tiffany will find no trouble, I'm sure.*"

The comm went silent.

Eric's eyes widened and his heart raced.

He could feel it. Maybe this wasn't the loop, but this was the solution.

—

Carl's breakfast was a bowl of glop that suggested someone had left yogurt out in the sun, then refrigerated it in a dank cave. There was no spoon. It was either lick it off his fingers or slurp, and this was neither the most lickable nor the most slurpable substance in the galaxy.

He glanced at the guard who'd just given that bowl its shove. "Thanks."

"Eat. You need strength."

"I'll be fine," Carl assured the guy. But he'd been watching. The government hadn't put together this spectacle overnight, and he had enough of an ear for eyndar that he'd been catching bits and pieces of conversations as the guards crossed paths with one another in his vicinity. "You're Angara, right?"

Carl With No Tastebuds used two fingers to scoop a wad of the gunk into his mouth.

"I don't need my name in your mouth, human. Swallow your stew."

Stew? That's what that crud was supposed to be?

Carl sucked the slop from the insides of his cheeks to get rid of the filmy after-feel. "Look, pal. This place is all P-tech. I know they're not listening in. You know it better than I do. So let's cut the acts."

"Eat," Angara ordered.

Obligingly, Carl took another finger scoop of the sludge. "Hey, I know how it is. Got three kids of my own. Two of them college brats. Like your Juko."

"You know nothing!"

"I know that your people don't offer free education. What it feels like to choose between your kids' futures and your own."

Angara scowled. His muzzle curled to expose one fang.

"I bet for the cost of this whole pageant Emperor Grudrak is throwing, they could pay off your college bills."

"You should be honored, then, human scum."

Carl left his bowl on the slab of a bed and walked up to lean on the bars. "No. Emperor Grudrak is the one being honored here. Not me. Not you. Sure as hell not Juko. But I could fix that."

Angara barked a laugh, though Carl could tell he was holding back so as not to draw others to investigate. He had the eyndar's attention. "You would say anything."

"I would *do* anything. More importantly, I would *pay* anything."

Angara shook his head. "Sad. Poor, broke human wants to buy his way out of death."

"What good is money otherwise? And I *used to be* broke. I've got money. Check the public filings for the Martian-based megacorp Harmony Bay. Their latest shareholder omni comm. Approval for a 5 percent stock transfer to acquire H-Tech Miracles. Which is me."

"Unlikely."

"Check for yourself. Dig. It's there if you look. But look quick. Today and tomorrow I get my ass chewed out by your people, then they start having fun killing me and bringing me back. Not sure what shape I might be in to help with my own escape by then."

"How can I believe a word you say?"

"Verify my story. Look, pal. I didn't live this long by going back on my word or betraying friends. You get me out of here, you're going to end up the rich friend of a very rich friend. Juko will get the best education, and you won't have to live in clan housing to afford it. I'm not going to lie and tell you it'll be easy, but if you decide you're in, I *do* have a foolproof plan. I just need an inside man, and you're the man for the job, Angara."

Angara showed that one fang again. "Eat your stew."

But as the guard turned to leave, Carl noted that he hadn't said "no."

It was the start of a plan, at least. Carl had little else to do but eat his Clam Snot Surprise and come up with that foolproof plan.

———

A fork fell with a clatter that rang through the dining lounge.

IT ALL STARTS HERE

And if Eric had any say in the matter, it was all going to end here, too. This loop. He felt it in his bones.

Five attempts with Emperor Khosrau's help had elicited

two responses from Aunt Tiffany before the reset. One was a harrowing warning that the eyndar had booby-trapped the sewers under the prison. Another warned of a patrol that would raise an alarm with a hair trigger and result in Dad's early execution.

How many more ways could this go wrong?

Eric timed his meal, sent in an order of tea for Sparta, and made his walk to Trebla's quarters, then whammied his friend and cousin to unblock comm access off the ship.

From there, Eric rushed back to his quarters and made the requisite comms to get in touch with Emperor Khosrau.

It amazed him, actually, how many different liaisons he could end up with through tiny variations in his routine. Yet somehow, the proper words would fire maneuvering pushies and nudge him back onto the right waterslide to end up with the emperor on the comm yet again.

The key points to the process, which he'd learned with some trials and tribulations...

Name-dropping Wizard Galantix would get him a connection to Azrael Copperfield, Guardian of the Plundered Tomes.

He had to get Azrael Copperfield to pass him along to Khosrau Blackstone, which meant Azrael needed to believe that Eric was Mort. Eric had enough practice by now that he might have been able to fool Mort into thinking Eric was him.

HOWEVER... Emperor Khosrau would only listen to Eric Ramsey, promiser of time favors, not Mordecai The Brown, extorter of secrets.

That got Eric to the proof of time loop, where he recounted a disturbing tale of Khosrau planning to marry Hadrian's cousin Euphrates MacGowan.

All that eventually got Eric to...

"*I see. And you presuppose that Tiffany Bell can carry out this rescue?*"

Eric recounted the whole plan Jessie had worked out as well as the two pieces of crucial intel that Tiffany had gathered herself and relayed back through the loop.

"... And if she fails, make sure she tells me what went wrong so we can learn better for next time."

"*You really have been looping time, haven't you?*"

"Yeah."

"*How many times has it been? How many times have we had some version of this same conversation?*"

Eric chuckled. "One more than last time you asked. But... a lot. We're getting really close."

"*All for that buffoon of a father of yours?*"

"I'd do anything to save him. So would Jessie. So would Mort. They don't know about the loop yet. Not in this loop. Neither of them takes it well when they find out. I'd appreciate it if you didn't try to contact them until Dad's safe."

"*Hmm... You suggest an interesting opportunity. The risk of failure seems minimal, and apparently there is no choice, ultimately, except success.*"

"That's the spirit."

"*As for what I desire in return...*"

"You name it. It's yours. Just hurry. If Aunt Tiffany leaves within the next three hours, she should be there in plenty of time."

One of these loops, Eric might have to get nosy about what exactly Khosrau was planning to ask. But this felt so close to right that he wasn't going to risk upsetting the launching of Aunt Tiffany's mission.

Maybe next loop.

The rest of the two-day loop was the hard part. Anxiety. Hope. And a sense of déjà vu that was off the charts. He felt like he'd learned all he needed, mentally documenting the trials and tribulations of two interminable days aboard the *Arete*. But if the Village of Eternity had taught him anything, it was patience.

And since he felt the end of the time loop coming on, he'd started trying to iron the wrinkles from as many lives as possible.

If nothing else, it was something to do.

Eric warned the Logistics team in the hangar that someone was planning to leak about their card games on duty.

He gave Makket a nudge to make inquiries that would let him discover Tippitak's pregnancy without ruining their marriage.

There was a meal that Daphne was going to love that Eric painstakingly programmed into the saloon food processor and left on the screen for her to discover and hit the PROCESS button.

He spilled every bit of juice that Britney might need to know about Harmony and hinted to Harmony that finding a babysitter and getting to know her new assistant in the off hours might be a good long-term boss action. This was one whose outcome he'd never been able to see due to the resets.

Jessie got advice on the mission, but nothing too suspicious. Eric just reminded her that he could be useful from time to time, and that felt good—as a screw-up little brother more so than as a wizard.

Eric avoided Hadrian. Not that he needed to go out of his way. But Eric was tiptoeing through the minefield of time, and Hadrian had rather big stompy boots when it came to magic. Simply not seeking his old mentor out generally kept their interactions to a minimum.

Charlotte got her half of a pair of new matching pajamas. Eight loops he'd worked to find the right style and color, but she was always so open and frank about what she liked and disliked that Eric narrowed it down quicker than most of the other tasks in his daily Samaritan routine. And it was a cut that he'd never have conjured up on his own, either, with loose flowy bits and snug, showy bits and a fabric that it didn't take magic to see through. And after yet another confession that he couldn't take them to the Village of Eternity just then, they played checkers long into the night before collapsing in snuggly exhaustion, pajamas discarded.

The one variable Eric couldn't seem to control, though he could tame it somewhat, was Sparta.

By the end of the second day of the loop, she met him in the hangar and accepted a thermal mug of C-K tea that he was asking to be made stronger every few loops. Makket had begun questioning whether he was going to be a party to murder, but Eric assured him that the intended drinker had a prodigious tolerance for the stuff.

"They're gone?" Sparta asked.

"Yeah. Same as always."

"No. I don't think it is."

"Is what?"

"The same as always..."

⬜

Astral space was still too gray for her liking. Jessie watched the control panel of Grosstet's Shuttle 1, perched on her human ergonomic adapter seat and interpreting standard units that she knew the machinery was converting from haathee equivalents at some unknown level of accuracy.

"Hey, relax, the hard part was getting off the ship," Hadrian told her. "I let Trebla in on the secret of my identity on the off chance it came down to a vote of no confidence in you. No way that walking shower clog was going to stab me in the back knowing the dirt I have on him. But here we are. Eight point whatever-the-hell-you-said astral units deep, and... we've got to be nearly to our destination by now. Don't we?"

Jessie peered at the ever-changing numbers on the readouts. "Yeah," she replied distractedly.

"Well, say the word, and I'll have us—"

"The word is WAIT. You may think your end of this deal is handled, but mine requires some fucking finesse. I've got to match course and speed with a tumbling planet that's outside our direct frame of reference, using maps we stitched together ourselves, then ballpark the rate of our astral re-entry so we don't go off course while we transition. Getting back to realspace is quicker than the transit to this shallow-ass deep astral, right?"

"Naturally," the wizard replied as if it were the most obvious statement. Like Jessie were asking whether planets orbited stars.

"How much quicker?"

"Very."

"Gimme a number I can count in my head."

"You want it quick as a blink, that's how fast you'll get it."

"No fuzzling?"

"I rarely fuzzle what I don't want to anymore. Eric is a klutz and Sparta—Athena love her—is a weakling. Charlotte is barely a wizard at all. Our leisurely descent was a consideration of your sensitive stomach for astral travel, not a limitation on my mastery. The ship ought to be fully functional after a near instantaneous return to the land of sewer pipes and pollution."

"Can you handle a 'wait for it, wait for it, NOW' kind of warning?"

Hadrian smirked. "I didn't know you had the chops to go with such a classic choice. I'd be delighted to infuse this Wax-i-Rod mission of yours with a little watercolor flair."

Jessie nudged them gently into position. But it was more akin to shooting pool on a ship with a faulty gravity stone during maneuvers. Everything in her frame of reference was in motion, including Shuttle 1. Any sense of motionlessness would, in fact, be an intricate balance of conflicting orbital and rotational motions.

"Wait for it... waaaaaiiiit for iiiiiit... NOW!"

The shuttle was back in realspace before Jessie could process that her stomach felt like it had been left at the top of a lift shaft when she stepped off at the ground floor. Turning aside, she heaved up her pre-mission snack.

"This is why we don't do that," Hadrian explained. "However. By the murk and drear, I imagine we've hit our mark."

Stomach convulsing with aftershocks, Jessie managed to confirm the supposition. "Yeah. Looks like we made it."

With a little swooping gesture with one index finger, there was a sizzle and crackle. The puddle of vomit was gone. Not a system on Shuttle 1 so much as blinked.

Hadrian gave her a grim, reassuring nod. "Let's go get Carl back."

━━

Transit through the sewage treatment center went smoothly. Jessie followed the map from her TeleJack, which had come through its magical transits like a champ. Quick, quiet murders, followed by discreet removal of incriminating bodies.

But whereas Jessie went to the trouble of hurling her fallen victims into the festering murk of black water, Hadrian just snapped his fingers and someone was gone.

"That... that was an illusion, right?" Jessie asked, shaken. "There was... I mean... You're just messing with me to prove a point. He wasn't really...?"

"There one second. Gone the next. And I didn't send him forward in time like I've heard Eric's done. That guy's not coming back. Ever. Now, if you'll save your demonstrations of awe for later, let's get moving."

When they hit the city streets, the pair found a party to rival Mardi Gras. Just as Eric had predicted they might, the eyndar had transformed the capture of Carl Ramsey into a celebration worthy of turning out the populace into the streets. It made no sense; it was an old war, one the Eyndar Empire often liked to pretend either hadn't happened or they won. But Eric had a penchant for thinking along with madness.

Prepared with alternate routes, Jessie avoided getting them sucked into the inexorable flow and ventured back through the waste facility and out a side exit.

Towering vid boards replayed a loop of Carl center stage at a kangaroo trial, shackled in place as the testimonials of so-called "victims" assailed him. The screens were everywhere. Large. Small. On the sides of apartment buildings and on the sides of public transports. Up direction posts and over businesses. In quieter times, Jessie could imagine these carried various adverts, but tonight they were recapping highlight-reel footage of human humiliation.

It didn't take long before they found the prison.

No justice without blood.

It seemed many eyndar citizens were sick of the government playing with its food. They wanted Carl dead, and they wanted him dead sooner rather than later. A cordon of police kept the crowd at bay, but who knew for how much longer.

Hadrian pressed forward, and some unseen, indescribable aura suggested that anyone in his path get out of it in a hurry.

At the steps, a flick of Mort's wrist ended the guards' feeble attempts to ascertain his identity or purpose in visiting. Clearly too important to impede, the pair were allowed entry with little fuss.

"State your business," a prison bureaucrat instructed brusquely.

Mort's eyndar was impeccable, even if his accent leaned Back Bay Bostonian. "We're here to see the human."

They'd been planning to sneak around and come in on a basement level, but Hadrian was clearly improvising; Jessie found herself unwilling to go against the judgment of such an experienced operative.

Odd as it was, with him in a body several years younger than her own.

"There are no visitors allowed. Only guards and medical staff are permitted access. Begone."

Hadrian pulled down his mask so that his eyes met those of the astonished administrator before she could raise an alarm. "Make an exception."

Canine eyes glazed over. Pupils shrank all the way shut. "Yes. I will. Summon. An escort."

Moments later, they had an escort and were headed down ancient duracrete steps toward the VIP cells.

This was all too easy.

Down.

Down.

Past the guards on patrol and doors leading into other cell blocks on levels closer to the surface.

Near the bottom, a commotion rose.

Panicked eyndar shouts of confusion revealed nothing but a security breach in progress.

"Shall we?" Mort asked in plain English.

Jessie gave him a nod.

With the wave of a hand, their escorts, already startled by the use of the human language, vanished in a flash of smoke. When the wizard, under a head of steam more ego than competence, tried to take the lead, Jessie demanded, "Do you know where you're going?"

Rather than answer in words, Mort stepped aside and allowed her to take point.

"Intruder!"

"Sound the alarm!"

"Lock down the building!"

"So much for getting to him first," Jessie griped, breaking into a run that slowed only to punch and kick steel-barred doors that blocked their path.

As Jessie blazed forward, exiting onto the level where they were keeping Carl prisoner, Hadrian lagged, fending off guards as they got anywhere near him. There were going to be a lot of no-call, no-shows for work around this place tomorrow, she mused darkly.

But her gallows humor vanished, replaced with a shot of adrenaline.

There was Dad's cell. And there was a body on the floor of it.

In no mood to wait for permission from man or God, she kicked open the door, lock be damned, and raced inside.

There was little doubt. A charred blaster hole in the middle of the chest was a heart shot.

It had hit hers as well.

"No... NO!!!" she wailed.

Hadrian skidded to a halt outside the cell. He saw. He knew. Jessie could see it in his eyes.

No time to waste, Jessie gathered up her father's body and slung it over her shoulder, grunting at the amount of beer she must have been lugging in addition to the necessary human anatomy.

"Clear us a path. We're getting him back to the *Arete*. Maybe Harmony can still fix this."

━━━

Jessie had been around a grouchy Enzio Stiles. She'd witnessed the pique of a miffed Hadrian The Brown when it was still him in that body.

But with Mordecai The Brown in charge of their escape from the eyndar homeworld, she witnessed true fury from a wizard for the first time.

Not a vid board was lit by the time Jessie got outside.

Crashed hovers littered the streets.

Terrified howls echoed through the canyons of skyscrapers with eyndar fleeing as fast as their feet could move.

Despite the night and the utter lack of technology, there was no shortage of light. Everything was on fire.

A city made of duracrete and iron and grime had become a smoky, oily torch that spared no one and nothing. Jessie tried to count the buildings that were, despite being made of purportedly fireproof materials, blazing and even melting away under the heat.

Overhead, a squad of civil patrol ships made a flyby, probably to do an intel sweep to figure out what the hell was happening. But six of them, flying in formation, suddenly all veered toward a central point and smashed together. Debris from the ground ranging from the chassis of hovers to dead eyndar bodies leapt into the air as if falling into a newly formed neutron star.

A ball of wreckage and carnage formed, hanging in midair, shrinking amid metallic shrieks and creaks, when all at once *that* burst into fresh flames. With a flick of Hadrian's hand, a streaking meteor rocketed toward the imperial palace, where it exploded, instantly engulfing the ornate stone edifice.

"Come on," the wizard cajoled her. "I didn't do that for you to gawk at. We need to get to the shuttle."

"Shuttle. Right." Checking her wrist, Jessie found, unbelievably, that her TeleJack still worked. Dad's weight made it awkward, but she managed to summon Shuttle 1 on autopilot. Unless the eyndar were growing civil defense patrol ships on trees, they were going to need time for more to arrive. Actually, if they *were* growing ships on trees, they'd need to import them to this barren, desolate object lesson of how bad Earth could have gotten if not for Black Ocean colonies.

Five minutes later, they were aboard Grosstet's shuttle.

Five more, and they were back aboard the *Arete*.

Shuttle 1 had commed ahead. Eric had eavesdropped, but he'd never gotten good enough at it to pick up the wording of the message. But it sounded urgent, and urgent was always bad.

Knowing he had a smidgen of time, Eric made his way to the lift doors.

Sparta hadn't waited around this time though. She rarely did. Like Hadrian, she was squirrelly from loop to loop, but she never outright interfered—at least, as far as he could tell.

Jessie piloted the shuttle through the floorcefield and over to the lift. He'd seen her do it enough to know her flying. The shuttle landed with the ramp toward the door.

This wasn't right. This wasn't right at all. What the heck? Aunt Tiffany was wrecking timeline after timeline with her efforts, and this was the first loop since she'd gotten involved that Jessie and Hadrian had been the ones to discover Dad's body. Hopefully she found a way to contact the *Arete* before the loop reset again; Eric needed to know what went wrong.

But he also needed to know what Jessie and Hadrian had encountered on the eyndar homeworld.

Chaotic, random loop results were the worst. At best, it meant he'd made a mistake and not noticed. At worst, some part of his intricate model of the ship and its inhabitants' actions of the loop's two-day duration were somehow no longer accurate.

He didn't want to write off this whole, oh-so-promising loop without a fight.

The lift doors opened. Britney and Harmony had a hover stretcher. Jessie flopped Dad onto it and followed the pair back into the lift. Eric knew the timing to the second and stepped on with ease.

"Can you do anything?" Jessie demanded.

Harmony was a flurry of handheld doodads. "No vitals. No heart rate. No brain activity. No... wait a second. What did you bring me?"

"My father!" Jessie snapped. "Get working! Bring him back!"

Harmony shook her head. "This isn't what you think it is."

Before their eyes, Dad's body rippled. Changed. Became someone else. Lying on the stretcher when the doors opened at the end of the lift ride was an eyndar in a prison guard's uniform with the same mortal wound in the center of his chest.

"Who? What? HOW?" Jessie demanded in a perplexed tizzy. "Where is my father?"

A slow, tentative smile spread on Eric's face.

Where, indeed?

He had some ideas.

———

Tiffany Bell's latest purchase had been a starship little bigger than a pilot's chair and a gap behind the seat for a duffel bag. No fancy amenities. No fucking star-drive. Low power. Cheap to fuel. Technically, it was an intracity commuter hover, but it was vacuum tight, and she'd paid for an upgrade to the nav system. While she'd been tempted by the cotton-candy pink, given her line of work, she chose a matte-black exterior instead.

But the interior was definitely cotton-candy-pink leather.

"Get to the Eyndar Empire homeworld, he says," Tiffany griped as she swung her duffel and arrested its arc such that it slumped down into the back of her ship.

"There's a prison across from the imperial palace, he says," she continued as she hopped over the sidewall and into the pilot's chair.

Nobody who knew her would have described Tiffany Bell as a large woman, and only someone making a serious effort to kiss her ass would have called her petite. Yet she had to take out her high ponytail when the cockpit canopy closed her in.

"Wonder if I ought to ask for a pay raise."

She was accustomed to getting dispatched all over the galaxy to kill people. To bring back books that neither they nor anyone else ought to have ever written. But saving people was *not* her thing. Saving Carl Ramsey was, unbelievably, *less* her thing.

Guy just needed to clench a little and shit out another lucky horseshoe.

As Tiffany lifted off, she realized the unfortunate truth: *she* was the latest in a long line of misused equestrian footwear.

There was no justice in this galaxy.

Orbital control didn't hassle Tiffany Bell. Not only was her new little toy registered as a Convocation vehicle with every exemption on the book, Vincente had casually mentioned that she'd be receiving an extra wide berth for her exit vector.

Earth traffic parted like the Red Sea before her.

Imperial orders.

Khosrau may have been a horny little dipshit with too high an opinion of his own magic, but he *did* have a knack for getting things done. That knack, of course, was named Vincente. Still, Tiffany wouldn't have wanted to trade places with the emperor. She could have. She'd turned down the job once, and she could have taken it by force from this pale imitation of the previous occupant of that body.

Tiffany didn't even bother clearing her astral transit with the authorities. Consequences happened to other people. She controlled her own fate, even if that weaselly Eric Ramsey was feeding them intel to suggest that Tiffany had fucked this up a few times already.

Not reassuring.

Not in the least.

If she was going to be living the day over and over, it might have been nice to know in advance. Picking out a dude the night before and starting off each loop of time with a good lay wouldn't have hurt. But no. She'd spent the morning doing paperwork at the library.

Deep.

Realspace plummeted away.

Gray, purple, and crimson astral whizzed by.

Tiffany shut her eyes to avoid seeing places that mortal eyes weren't meant to witness. Also, the swirling patterns in the borderline imperceptible colors gave her a headache.

Once the nav computer came back to life, she nudged the

ship the equivalent of a city block or two. This far down, that was all it took.

A little closer.

Space returned to red, and she signaled that she was ready to stop here.

The nav computers awoke from another tech nap, and Tiffany dialed in a more precise location. Planetside. Inland. Didn't much matter where.

Realspace.

Whoops! Gravity.

In and out of astral all the time, it was easy to forget that gravity existed. Out in orbit or beyond any proximate gravity wells, it was easy to ignore.

Tiffany winced as her ship—her brand-new, still-smelled-like-the-air-fresheners-trying-to-make-old-ships-smell-new starship—slammed into the turf of a factory town behind a wire fence.

Eyndar came her way, yammering, blabbering, waving arms. Tiffany was uninjured in the fall and ungrateful for what she imagined were offers of help that would evaporate the instant she was identified as human.

She let them get close.

A veil of fog rose at her summons.

Five bodies hit some kind of primitive tarmac material. A sixth eyndar blubbered something as she backed away from the angry, pitiless human.

Until she couldn't.

Tiffany held the factory worker motionless. "Sorry," she said, using the Golden Tongue. "I don't understand eyndar well enough on my own. Going to need a translator."

Without ceremony, Tiffany plunged two fingers through the eyndar woman's eyes. When they came out, her fingers were gritty with ash.

Hastily undressing the worker, Tiffany shrugged out of her own clothes and inspected the body in detail. Moments later, Tiffany herself was eyndar and wriggling into the worker's uniform.

ID.

Datapad.

Tool belt.

Cash—in banags.

She could read the datapad now, too.

This wasn't her first time in an eyndar body. The fur took getting used to, especially the rub of it against the fabric of her clothes. But other than that, she didn't mind it so much.

Retrieving her duffel bag from the ship, Tiffany made the vessel disappear via invisibility and the bodies disappear via fire.

It took her thirty minutes or so, and a barked excuse to her persona's supervisor about a womanly medical problem, but Tiffany made her way to the factory town's major transit hub and booked passage to the capital.

———

How could any self-respecting species not know how to fucking name places? Tiffany's tram stopped places with names that translated to Eastern Farm Town, Deepwater Port, and Sheep Slaughterhouse. The capital city of the whole fucking empire was just Capital.

Also, despite dressing like a shipping sack and not even having her fur styled, she fielded eight offers of casual sex during the trek.

Someone just needed to burn this whole species to the ground and start over.

Thankfully, a little math and some window shopping once

she arrived at the capital was enough to determine Tiffany had the money for attire that wasn't obviously meant for on the job.

Feeling both too old *and* too wrong species, she picked out some festive club wear and hit the streets.

While the atmosphere was certainly festive, the eyndar themselves didn't know what to fucking do for a good time. No rhythm. Shitty music. Lighting only in shades their colorblind asses could tell apart. Tiffany had snuck into dance clubs as far back as middle school. With enough cosmo tint and a decent fake ID, most bouncers learned not to care. But this party wasn't worth anyone sneaking into.

Not without an ulterior motive, at least.

As she neared the capital's central plaza, the music faded. Audio now came from bereaved war widows and orphans. Old soldiers reminisced about battlefield crimes that had taken the lives of comrades.

Wow, they were really putting on a big-time show trial. Tiffany had heard enough conflicting stories from that time period to take anything these fuckers were saying with a grain of salt. Most of them probably *believed* their own shit. But who'd they get their intel from? The news? Official military reports? Feelings?

Tiffany joined the masses for a while, listening while munching on kip'baat, which she'd never gotten a look at the ingredients for but tasted like a cross between pepperoni and a cheese dog. Probably wouldn't have tasted as good with a human tongue, but she was borrowing a form that could appreciate heavy, greasy meats.

Her eyndar ears caught the proceedings more easily, too, even if her understanding of the language was still shabby.

Blah, blah, blah, took my little puppy away. Blah, blah, blah, ruined my family's chance for a legacy. What did the citizens of the Eyndar Empire expect? It was a war. She had to admit, though, they were making Carl out to be a pretty good scapegoat.

Look at him up there. Impassive. Almost bored. Like a tourist weathering a cultural performance and trying not to offend anyone.

One thing was for certain, she wasn't going to be extracting *anyone* from under the noses of what must have been a hundred thousand eyeballs in the plaza. Elevated on a little platform. No doubt being broadcast live across the empire. No. The timeline relayed by that fucking *rat* of a little chronomancer suggested that his own efforts taking on the whole plaza with the haathee at his side had resulted in disaster.

She had until tomorrow, and Tiffany was going to take it.

Time was a resource. She had a limited quantity if the loop mechanics were as rock solid as she'd been led to understand. But she couldn't rush and waste what she'd been allotted.

Citizens came and went. The less rabid among the spectators lingered near the back for easy egress, and Tiffany joined them after a while. She wasn't going to learn much more from the repetitive grievances as an interminable line of older eyndar aired them.

Instead, she scouted.

The military police headquarters was a refreshingly drab and utilitarian piece of historical architecture. Stoicism, as an imperial philosophy, embodied in a building. This had to be where they were keeping Carl between festival events.

Tiffany found the employee entrance around back, the prisoner transfer portal with its redundant layers of walls and gates, and the main entrance, which was the stupidest plan of the bunch.

In and out via the guard entrance was the way to go.

And, to make that easier, it was going to help knowing who had authorized access to that route.

Fortunately for Tiffany, eyndar were drinkers. Bars abounded here the way cafes did in Paris Prime. Or the way bars did in Boston. She got herself a window seat and watched the comings and goings while getting a light buzz from free drinks that amorous idiots purchased her.

No expert on eyndar tastes, Tiffany was discovering that her factory worker was something of a catch when re-clothed in something less utilitarian than coveralls. All the better.

She watched the gates.

She watched the chronos.

At the local equivalent of dinnertime, a small army of guards filed into the building. As soon as they'd finished clearing the streets outside, a similar contingent poured forth, dispersing back to their daily lives after a long shift.

Some of them came to the bar.

One of them came to her table.

"Share a drink, short fur?" the guard asked with narrowed, predatory eyes.

"Depends," Tiffany replied. She used the Golden Voice since her accent sucked. It was rare for anyone but a wizard to even notice. "I'm here for the celebration. Are you in a mood to celebrate?"

A wolfish grin hit his features. "Sure am. Just did a cycle underground. I'm ready to cut loose. I'm Dangar."

Tiffany recalled the ID from her factory badge. "Traxa."

The pair drank and chatted. Dangar regaled her with tales of notorious prisoners and boasts of his sexual prowess that made his intentions for the evening quite clear. Tiffany did nothing to disabuse him of any notion of what she might be willing to do. Her every flirtation and tease suggested she was a side-town girl in the capital for a good time with the first manly man to come along and show her one.

Atrocious as the conversation might have been, Tiffany had heard far worse. The worst thing this guy might have had in mind was taking her, willing or not, and leaving her for dead afterward—and even that seemed like a stretch for this guy. He seemed more hot air than truly dangerous. On other assignments, Tiffany had been promised immortality as a statue in a rose garden, threatened with having her soul shredded to ribbons and kept in the gems of a tiara, and had it explained to her exactly how her mind was going to be reduced to idiocy to make her a willing slave.

Dangar was an amateur.

Plus, the beer was fine.

(Cheapskate)

They headed back to Dangar's place. It was a small apartment overlooking a pair of dumpsters for the buildings to either side of an alley. Based on the decor, the flatpics, and the double-wide bed, it was clear the guard didn't live here alone.

Dangar must have noticed her deduction. "Nothing to worry about. My mate hates the crowds. She is staying with her sister."

Over the course of her career, Tiffany had made peace with many pragmatic aspects of her line of work. She'd dug around in the innards of more creatures than she cared to count, sentient and otherwise. She'd seen the light leave enough eyes to spectate an eyndar execution. She'd smelled the entrails and offal of beasts that never should have existed. But, generally speaking, she didn't fuck anyone for professional advantage anymore.

Dangar's tongue fished around Tiffany's mouth like she needed help cleaning peanut butter from between her teeth.

Stupidly long tongues had far better uses, but she wasn't going to let this go on too much longer, so she played along.

Cloth ripped as the guard removed Tiffany's newly purchased clothes, which were suited better to displaying fur than rough handling. Planning ahead, Tiffany was far more cautious with the guard's uniform, though she needn't have worried, thanks to much sturdier fabrics.

Face to face. Tongues wrapped together in knots. Totally unclothed. Tiffany was, thanks to cultural qualms, still fairly safe, even as their bodies touched.

When, with an amorous snarl, Dangar threw Tiffany to the bed, face down, she knew it was time to put an end to the charade. Dangar fell atop her, but Tiffany had rolled onto her back at the last second before he pinned her.

Using the space afforded them on the extra wide marital bed, she rolled atop the eyndar and straddled his torso. By the wide pupils and a nagging poke at her lower back, Tiffany knew the guard didn't realize his peril.

Her hands closed around the eyndar's throat. At first, he played along, even. Then, the gasping. The soundless flapping of the jaw. The scratching at arms suddenly made of iron.

When Dangar lost consciousness, she released her grip and flipped him over, facedown on the bed. Mounting him again, she squeezed harder. Tiffany held on and counted. Then, squeezing a little more for good measure, cracked the windpipe.

As she donned Dangar's uniform, it fit as well as it had its former owner. With a minor exception, anyway. And on the bed, an amorous encounter gone wrong. Poor Traxa should have been more careful who she went home drunk with. With her neck broken and clothing scattered, it wouldn't take a crack investigative team to make that conclusion. The only way to have staged the scene more convincingly, Tiffany couldn't manage. Not with how she'd modified this borrowed body.

All she could hope was that no one walked in on her at the communal pissing post in the prison tomorrow.

Of course, one other complication presented itself. She wasn't due back on shift at the prison until morning. And going out on the street as Dangar posed a whole host of problems in the meantime.

Tiffany spent the night on Dangar's couch.

━━━

No one challenged her entry into the military prison when Tiffany showed up for work the next day in Dangar's body.

The prison building felt its age. Horror and despair had seeped into the stonework via the sweat and tears of countless prisoners. A faint reek of harsh industrial cleaners suggested the blood and excrement was rinsed away with regularity.

They were a sullen, hung-over workforce. What little chatter was required of her, Tiffany supplied via the Golden Voice.

Down in a locker room one level below the street, Tiffany found Dangar's name and quietly forced open a tumbler lock to access his belongings. She exchanged his personal blaster for a suit of scienced-up armor fabric reminiscent of an ancient dog-training bite suit, which privately amused her no end.

Before closing the locker, however, Tiffany took a surreptitious glance at her colleagues, then slipped the blaster into the front of her pants.

Two problems solved at once. She was armed, and her pants fit slightly more the way they'd have fit the real Dangar.

Not that Tiffany *needed* a blaster to be dangerous. But she'd had a long night on a shitty couch to plan things, and just as she'd murdered Dangar, she'd have liked a chance to at least delay a proper investigation with a wild goose chase.

Eyndar were just over-evolved wolves, anyway. They should have *loved* chasing geese.

Tiffany received Dangar's daily assignment, and she leaned on her designated partner for guidance.

They were patrolling the dissidents block, not the VIPs down in the lowest level. Bad luck, but Tiffany had gotten names of the ones at the very lowest levels, the ones with the assignment she'd have preferred. If things went badly, and this turned out to really be a time loop, at least she could make an attempt to relay the names of the day's randomly assigned Carltenders.

Dangar had been low-hanging fruit, but that didn't mean Tiffany couldn't climb a tree if the mission called for it.

She bided her time. The day wore on. She had a number in her head, a rough estimate of when Carl might have been killed before someone got here to try their own amateur methods to extract him. Her own blood pressure rose.

There were a million ways to calm a mind. Tiffany didn't want hers calmed. She relished the tension, the crisp, clear sense of *living* that came with such a state. She could have hooked up with a dude, squeezed out a couple kids for him, and whiled away her life on a couch, eating her way through the Friendli Foods product directory as she binged holovid romances.

She lived for the thrill.

Khosrau, slutty man-child that he was, came up with interesting shit he wanted done and didn't care how. This mission was a masterpiece, a featured chapter in a memoir that —if she admitted it—Tiffany was probably never going to get around to writing.

And the parts she was *definitely* going to skip were these interminable waits between the interesting bits, when feet that weren't even hers were sore and she needed to take a piss but had to time it for when she was able to sneak off alone.

Another of the guards came by just after Tiffany and her partner's turn on lunch break.

"Hey, they're taking turns pissing on the human," their fellow guard informed them. "Keep it quiet, but you can sign up by word of mouth."

If they had Carl back in custody already, that meant that the window had opened on his murder. The parade of the aggrieved had run its course, and there was nothing but a wait until morning for the torture and reversible executions to begin.

"Good way to celebrate since we can't get out to see, right?" Tiffany's partner suggested.

They both gave their names and were told that coverage for their patrols was getting worked out on the side.

Bureaucracy, even in insubordination. Amazing.

Carl was soaked to the skin and his sense of smell had taken a sabbatical. He lay on the cot, staring at the uninteresting ceiling. He cocked one arm, fingers tucked behind his head, in an attempt to shield his face.

Footsteps approached.

"Rules are simple," Carl called out. "Anyone hits me in the face, I peek and reveal all your inadequacies to everyone who comes after. Hit nothing but floor, and I'll tell your buddies you're packing stuunji equipment down there."

"You really are a sorry sight," the latest guard told him.

Carl might have been a miserable, sore, stiff, exhausted, soaking, reeking mess, but he also recognized English with a mid-core accent over the weak attempts the occasional eyndar guards made.

Except, when he lifted his head, it *was* an eyndar outside his cell. "OK. I'll bite. Who's behind that fur?"

"Well, fuckwad, at least your mind isn't gone."

"Tiffany?" he guessed.

The eyndar snickered. "God, with this nose, you are just... It's almost indescribable."

"Are you here to gloat, finish me off, or get me out of here?"

"Hadn't really considered it, but I suppose one and three."

Carl was on his feet as fast as creaky old bones could manage. "Mind a quick, magical liquid removal service?"

"Oh, you weren't getting a choice," Tiffany assured him.

That was about the time that Carl noticed a second guard standing behind her, staring with unseeing eyes. "Who's your friend?"

Spreading his arms, he allowed a magical suction to vacuum away all the urine to which he'd been subjected to of late. It became a wobbly, zero-G-looking globule, far larger than he'd have expected, considering evaporation.

In her eyndar guise, but using her own voice, Tiffany hooked a thumb at the other guard. "Don't you recognize him?"

Carl squinted. "Dangar? No. You're Dangar. Who's that?"

"You."

Tiffany turned, yanking a blaster from her crotch in one smooth motion and firing it.

The cell door swung open. Carl and the guard exchanged outward appearances at the threshold. But the blaster hole remained where it belonged.

"Time to cause a little trouble to cover our escape."

"Thanks. I'll owe you one. Didn't expect you'd be the one coming for me."

Tiffany nodded soberly. "I... don't think I was the original plan."

"I could have flown, you know," Carl mentioned offhandedly as Tiffany brought them in for a landing.

"Yeah," Tiffany agreed without giving the matter any real thought. Of course, Carl could have flown. He was a pilot more so than any other profession at which he'd toiled. Two-bit smuggler. Birthday-party-grade guitarist. Insubordinate naval officer. Flying was all he did well.

The comm crackled. *"Convocation vessel, you are cleared for an assisted landing vector in Boston Prime restricted airspace."*

"Thanks, Orbital Control," Tiffany replied. "Appreciate the quick work. I'll just—" She slapped away Carl's hand as he reached past her. "I'll—" She turned and gave him a shove, wondering how much magic this ridiculous contraption could handle if she wanted him more thoroughly restrained.

"If I could just—"

"Stop it—"

"Yeah, but—"

"Is there a problem, Convocation vessel?"

Shit. "No. No problem. Just a passenger eager to get home and with poor comm manners." When she pulled back her arm, Carl rubbed his throat.

"Why'd you have to be like that?" he asked. "I just wanted to check on outbound traffic, see if I could wheedle a priority departure vector while you had the guy on the comm handing out exemptions."

He slumped into his seat in the back.

This wasn't Tiffany's new hover.

They'd purloined this vehicle from outside a parade cordon as a riot started in the eyndar capital. Apparently, someone had started a rumor that the human prisoner was dead, and the public had been denied the spectacle. That rumor raced ahead of the ones who'd started it, and in the chaos, they'd taken a residential model spacebound.

Now, thankfully within an atmosphere again, the rickety family transport jetted down on a laser course for Boston Prime.

"It's almost pretty from up here," Tiffany commented, looking to break the ice on a new conversation.

"Almost a lot of things. Almost free. Almost affordable. Almost worth a visit. But it's only almost; it isn't any of them. Nice if you can get free entry vectors, though."

"Don't even try it. That code—"

"Changed by next week. I know. I know."

"Try already changed. It was single use. The Convocation doesn't fuck around." Tiffany kept her hands firmly on the controls. Much as she knew how to fly and did it all the time, she couldn't just casually not watch where she was going. They'd already veered slightly off their approved approach vector while he was distracting her. If they hadn't been in keepout airspace, there might have been a collision.

When they reached the palace grounds, Tiffany was the first one down the ramp. Armed imperial guards swarmed them.

"Strip it for parts for all I care," Tiffany told them. She gestured to Carl. "This one's with me."

"Yes, Wizard Tiffany."

"Wow," Carl commented as he puppy-dogged at her heels. "You really came up in the galaxy while I wasn't looking."

"I'm what your friend Mort used to be, minus the bureaucratic shit that Azrael handles. It's symbiotic. He guards me against papercuts and meetings; I let him stay cozy on Earth without seeing the sausage-making process of bringing in new literature. You're lucky you've made friends, because on your own, you're kind of nothing. It's amazing there was this much fuss over you."

"What can I say? I bring out the best in people. Now... if you wouldn't mind directing me to a public terminal, I wouldn't mind getting word back to my family that I'm not the main course at a feast in Emperor Grudrak's name."

"Sorry, Emperor Khosrau was particular about keeping you safely out of sight until his people make certain the political cover is in place. Technically, Earth Empire just carried out a military operation on the Eyndar Empire's homeworld."

"Emperor Khosrau, huh?" Carl echoed with a wink. "Gotcha."

Tiffany pulled up short. "That? Right there? That's why you don't get unsupervised comm use without clearance."

A pair of Khosrau's personal guards marched up. "Wizard Tiffany, you're requested at the Library of the Plundered Tomes. We've been ordered to escort the hostage to Emperor Khosrau."

"Technically, I wasn't a hostage," Carl piped up. "That would have implied they were using me for leverage and that I could be bargained for. I was a convicted criminal under their kooky, politically convenient laws, and I'm an even bigger hero under ours, now, I think."

"Whatever," Tiffany replied, exasperated. "He's your problem now. Have fun, flyboy. Say hi to your kids for me, and tell Eric if he does this again, I'll kill him."

Carl laughed. "Yeah. He gets that a lot."

━

They'd moved the dead eyndar to Med Bay. A grim gathering surrounded the examination table.

"I want answers." This was Jessie's opening salvo in a larger argument to come. "I carried someone one point six kilometers through a fucking war zone, and that doesn't count five flights of steps. When I picked him up, it was Bradley Carlin Ramsey, my father—my late father, it was looking like. Now, it's some fucking eyndar nobody."

Harmony took it from here. "The deceased is an eyndar male, aged approximately 28 years. Based on muscle structure and callusing, he worked a job with moderate physical demands. He shows evidence of numerous minor injuries that didn't require medical attention by eyndar standards. The lack of more severe injuries or enhanced muscle structures suggests that he was not a frontline combatant. He was adequately fed and groomed. Neurochemical analysis shows a baseline moderate stress. This is consistent with a prison guard more so than an inmate."

"Someone magicked him," Hadrian declared. "And they did it with enough subtlety that I didn't notice until I looked for it. Surely not in the heat of a rescue."

"Fine. Someone magicked up a corpse to look like Dad," Jessie stated. "Here's the million-terra question: where did Dad end up?"

Daphne shook her head. "Newsfeeds are exploding across the Eyndar Empire. If they still have him, they're willing to tear themselves to pieces over his loss. They're tying it to rebels responsible for assassinating Emperor Grudrak."

Jessie's jaw clenched. "We spent weeks planning this mission. We risked our lives and risked making ourselves a priority target for the entire Eyndar Empire. More than we even already were—"

"In for a penny, and all that," Mindy muttered.

"And we don't even know where he is now?" Jessie shouted. "Ideas? Anybody?"

Silence froze the crew in amber.

"That's our new mission. Find out what happened to Carl Ramsey between planning this mission and executing it. Senior staff in the Briefing Room at 0900 tomorrow morning, and I want theories plus actionable plans to test them. Dismissed."

At the back of the assemblage, Eric Ramsey slunk away.

———

Mort indulged in a long bath, sloughing off eyndar stench and the stress of an annoying day. In a way, the discovery of a ruse had come as a relief. He hadn't put much stock in little Harmony's necromantic skills. Mistress of dark sciences or not, the girl had her limits.

When he exited the tub in a bathrobe, allowing himself to drip everywhere rather than dry himself with magic, he heard the wall ringing.

Drat and be bothered, it was a comm. It had a telltale, nattering quality that none of the other tech gizmos duplicated. Walking up to the thing, he ordered it, "Turn on."

"*VOICE ACTIVATION ACCEPTED.*"

"Who's there?" Mort demanded.

"*You ought to be more polite, especially when speaking to your monarch,*" the wall replied.

Ah. So it was him. "You're my monarch in the way that Cedric is my son. A technicality, a legality, and an unfortunate and estranged fact."

"*I can see why you dropped debate. Those poor, tormented words. But I didn't contact you to suffer your verbal barbs.*"

"It's a bonus I throw in. Like the fries with your order of a Blaster Burger combo."

"*I have something you've lost. Or should I say... some... one.*"

"You're doing it creepy. I think you were going for melodrama. Take an acting class. They'd probably comp you, like a Friends and Emperors program at The Boston Institute of the Arts."

"*I have Carl Ramsey in my custody.*"

Mort didn't like that word custody. "Care" might have been nice. But "custody" had a certain authoritarian blemish he couldn't look past. And Khosrau may have been a fool, but he wasn't an idiot. "What could you possibly want for him? I've given you everything in the galaxy."

"*Have you? I'll gladly give you back your only true friend in this galaxy. But I have a price...*"

━━

Dinner was pancakes. Eric had gone with banana this time, mostly for the change of pace. Across from him, Charlotte shook her head at the sight as she dined on sushi. Eric had a hard time using chopsticks without magical help.

"Are you quite all right?" Charlotte asked between rolls. "You've taken your father's situation well enough, but you don't have to weather it stoically."

Stoicism had never been attributed to Eric before now. He cried at holovids where no one got killed. He mourned paper birds that got ruined in a puddle. If he put a cork in his feelings, they'd just escape out the open, broken end of the bottle.

"Dad's fine. I know he is."

"There's a line between optimism and delusion."

"I'm on the good side of it. Not really looking to explain why, but I'd know if he were dead."

"Does it have to do with Sparta Dahl?"

Eric glanced aside as he pondered whether or not it did. He'd discussed the time loop with her, but she'd been more of an impediment than a help. He'd have omitted her from the plan entirely if she hadn't gummed up the works every time he'd left her to her own ends.

Apparently, Eric took too long formulating his answer. "I wouldn't put too much stock in anything she foresees. Prophecy is self-defeating as often as it is self-fulfilling. They see alternate futures that are altered by merely glimpsing them."

"She seems pretty powerful. At oracling, that is."

"She's worse for her gift, not better. Clearer inaccuracies are all the more misleading. I don't doubt what she can see; I question the validity of taking action on any of it. She's only going to get—"

A fork fell with a clatter that rang through the dining lounge.

Eric stiffened.

"Sorry," Trebla called out. "Three left hands over here."

"You're awfully jumpy," Charlotte scolded. "You need to find a way to relax."

Eric glanced down.

His pancakes were still banana.

Tonight, he silently promised Charlotte with a meaningful look, they would visit the Village of Eternity. Then, Eric would relax.

BLACK OCEAN UNIVERSE

Black Ocean

Black Ocean is a vivid 26th century story universe where science and magic coexist—sort of.

Black Ocean: Galaxy Outlaws (16 missions)

Black Ocean: Galaxy Outlaws is a fast-paced fantasy space opera series about the small crew of the *Mobius* trying to squeeze out a living. If you love fantasy and sci-fi, and still lament over the cancellation of *Firefly*, *Black Ocean: Galaxy Outlaws* is the series for you.

Read about the *Black Ocean: Galaxy Outlaws* series and discover where to buy at: galaxyoutlawsmissions.com

Black Ocean: Astral Prime (12 missions)

Co-written with author M.A. Larkin, *Black Ocean: Astral Prime* hearkens back to location-based space sci-fi classics like *Babylon 5* and *Star Trek: Deep Space Nine*. *Astral Prime* builds on the rich *Black Ocean* universe, introducing a colorful cast of characters for new and returning readers alike. Come along for the ride as a minor outpost in the middle of nowhere becomes a key point of interstellar conflict.

Read about the *Black Ocean: Astral Prime* series and discover where to buy at: astralprimemissions.com

Black Ocean: Mercy for Hire (16 missions)

Black Ocean: Mercy for Hire follows the exploits of a pair of do-gooder bounty hunters who care more about saving the day than securing a payday. The series builds on the rich *Black Ocean* universe, centering on a couple of fan-favorites and introducing a colorful cast for new and returning readers alike. Fans of vigilante justice and heroes who exemplify the word will love this series.

Read about *Black Ocean: Mercy for Hire* and discover where to buy at: mercyforhiremissions.com

Black Ocean: Mirth & Mayhem (16 missions)

Black Ocean: Mirth & Mayhem delves into the origins of two vagabonds making their living among the stars. Mort is a wizard coming to grips with a life on the run and estrangement from the comforts and respect he had on Earth. Brad is an impressionable youth, too clever for his—or anyone's—good. And Chuck Ramsey is the mold that Brad's trying to break out of, which is harder than he could ever have dreamed.

Read about *Black Ocean: Mirth & Mayhem* and discover where to buy at: mirthandmayhemmissions.com

Black Ocean: Passage of Time (in-progress)

The year was 2586. A few minutes later, it was 2591. Caught up in a time travel snafu, Eric and Jessie Ramsey become fugitives from the people who want answers as to how they did it—and where their loyalties lie in the galactic war that broke out in their absence.

Read about *Black Ocean: Passage of Time* and discover where to buy at: passageoftimemissions.com

Black Ocean Fan Group

Join the *Black Ocean* Facebook fan group to discuss *Black Ocean* with other outlaws. Chat about ebooks, audio, or paper versions; main series or spin-offs; or share photos of the pet you named after Kubu.

Request to join at: blackoceanfans.com

Black Ocean Merch

Wish you could live in the Black Ocean world?

I can't promise you'll win an argument with the universe, but you CAN wear your own wizard hoodie (adorned with Convocation medallion), disguise your boring 21st-century soda or beer with the Earth's Preferred can cooler, or fly the Poet Fleet Jolly Roger.

Browse merch at: blackoceangear.com

Twinborn Chronicles

The *Twinborn Chronicles* is an epic fantasy saga based on the possibility that our dreams offer us a glimpse into the life of another – another who can get the same glimpse into our world.

Read about the *Twinborn Chronicles* and discover where to buy at: twinbornchronicles.com

Twinborn Chronicles: Awakening

Experience the journey of mundane scribe Kyrus Hinterdale who discovers what it means to be Twinborn—and the dangers of getting caught using magic in a world that thinks it exists only in children's stories.

Twinborn Chronicles: War of 3 Worlds

Then continue on into the world of Korr, where the Mad Tinker and his daughter try to save the humans from the oppressive race of Kuduks. When their war spills over into both Tellurak and Veydrus, what alliances will they need to forge to make sure the right side wins?

Project Transhuman: Eve14

Project Transhuman brings genetic engineering into a post-apocalyptic Earth, 1000 years aliens obliterated all life.

These days, even the humans are built by robots.

Charlie7 is the oldest robot alive. He's seen everything from the fall of mankind at the hands of alien invaders to the rebuilding of a living world from the algae up. But what he hasn't seen in over a thousand years is a healthy, intelligent human. When Eve stumbles into his life, the old robot finally has something worth coming out of retirement for: someone to protect.

Read about all of the *Project Transhuman* books and discover where to buy at: projecttranshuman.com

OTHER BOOKS BY J. S. MORIN

Sins of Angels

Co-written with author M.A. Larkin, *Sins of Angels* is an epic space opera series set 3000 years after the fall of Earth. With the scope of *Dune* and the adventurous spirit of *Indiana Jones*, it delivers a conflict that spans galaxies and rests on the spirit of brave researcher Professor Rachel Jordan. Follow the complete saga, and watch as the fate of our species hangs in the balance.

Read about *Sins of Angels* and discover where to buy at:
sinsofangelsbooks.com

Shadowblood Heir

Shadowblood Heir explores what would happen if the writer of your favorite epic fantasy TV show died before the show ended—and the show was responsible. If you wonder what it would be like if an epic fantasy world invaded our world, this urban fantasy story might give you that glimpse.

Read about *Shadowblood Heir* and discover where to buy at:
shadowbloodheir.com

EMAIL INSIDERS

You made it to the end! Maybe you're just persistent, but hopefully that means you enjoyed the book. But this is just the end of one story. If you'd like reading my books, there are always more on the way!

Perks of being an Email Insider include:

- Inside track on beta reading and advance review copies (ARCs)
- Access to Inside Exclusive bonus extras and giveaways
- Best of my blog about fantasy and science fiction topics

Sign up for the my Email Insiders list at: jsmorin.com/updates

ABOUT THE AUTHOR

I am a creator of worlds and a destroyer of words. As a fantasy writer, my works range from traditional epics to futuristic fantasy with starships. I have worked as an unpaid Little League pitcher, a cashier, a student library aide, a factory grunt, a cubicle drone, and an engineer—there is some overlap in the last two.

Through it all, though, I was always a storyteller. Eventually I started writing books based on the stray stories in my head, and people kept telling me to write more of them. Now, that's all I do for a living.

I enjoy strategy, worldbuilding, and the fantasy author's privilege to make up words. I am a gamer, a joker, and a thinker of sideways thoughts. But I don't dance, can't sing, and my best artistic efforts fall short of your average notebook doodle. When you read my books, you are seeing me at my best.

Connect with me online
jsmorin.com

facebook.com/authorjsmorin

bookbub.com/authors/j-s-morin

youtube.com/@authorjsmorin